Baden had never ▌▌▌▌▌▌▌
Twinkling stars in ▌▌▌▌
glory rained their ~~light~~ **down on**
them. Then he saw a streak moving
across the sky.

"Is that a comet?"

Kate turned to him, her face alive with excitement. "Yes."

He pulled her close, loving the way her curves fit into him. "It's a special night all round."

She laid her head on his shoulder. "One worth remembering."

Her quiet words unexpectedly speared him. *One* night. It was what they both wanted, what they had both agreed to. Neither of them was able to offer more. He couldn't risk loving again. He had to protect Sasha. Kids loved easily, but as Kate didn't want a relationship he couldn't risk Sasha getting attached. Another loss could devastate her.

But he had tonight. They had less than twelve hours before real life returned. Before he was a doctor again, before he was a father again. Before life returned to what it had been.

So why the hell was he out here looking at stars?

He swung Kate into his arms and took her back inside.

Dear Reader,

I live in a town where you are only one or two handshakes away from everyone. At times this has its disadvantages, but one of the overwhelming advantages is a sense of community. With that in mind, I created the Outback town of Warragurra. This town has its problems, but it also has its strengths, and when one of its own is under threat it draws together as a community, united in purpose.

Against this backdrop, Baden and Kate struggle with their attraction to each other. Baden and his daughter, Sasha, are recovering from loss and creating a new life. Kate is rebuilding her life and filling it with her work at the flying-doctors' base. Neither Kate nor Baden believe in happy-ever-afters, and they closely guard their hearts. But the Outback heat shimmers between them, and the township of Warragurra pushes them together until they finally realize that to risk loving is what life is all about.

I hope you enjoy your visit to Warragurra, and that you will join me again later in the year for another Warragurra story.

Love,

Fiona x

A WEDDING IN WARRAGURRA
Fiona Lowe

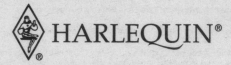

HARLEQUIN®

TORONTO • NEW YORK • LONDON
AMSTERDAM • PARIS • SYDNEY • HAMBURG
STOCKHOLM • ATHENS • TOKYO • MILAN • MADRID
PRAGUE • WARSAW • BUDAPEST • AUCKLAND

ISBN-13: 978-0-373-06644-5
ISBN-10:   0-373-06644-9

A WEDDING IN WARRAGURRA

First North American Publication 2008

www.eHarlequin.com

Printed in U.S.A.

A WEDDING IN WARRAGURRA

To my cousin, Annie, for her wholehearted
enthusiasm, unwavering support
and shelf-arranging skills. A woman going places
in her own life.

CHAPTER ONE

'But it isn't pink.'

Kate Lawson heard the disappointment in the young girl's voice as she browsed in the limited clothing section of Warragurra's answer to Teen Gear. She glanced up and just caught the woebegone expression that matched the voice before a set of very broad shoulders partially blocked her view.

'Not everything in life is pink or purple, Sasha.' The deep, melodious voice carried a smile.

Kate grinned, wishing she could see the man's face. Did he have a clue what he was up against? Shopping with tweens was a minefield. She knew only too well. She had a niece much the same age and a Girl Guide troop that kept her on her toes.

Sasha tossed her head and stuck a hand on her hip. 'I do know that, Dad.'

'So, perhaps it's time to branch out and explore green and blue now that you're twelve.' Patience threaded through the words. He picked up a cute striped vest top. 'What about this?'

Kate watched, fascinated and completely forgetting she was supposed to be finding a gift for her niece. That she was supposed to be ironing her nurse's uniform and polishing her shoes for her first day back at work. Not to mention the million other things that needed doing in preparation for her return to the real world of Warragurra. She'd been gone six months, but she couldn't hide for ever.

Sasha wrinkled her nose at the top that lay across her father's arm.

Long masculine fingers trailed across the fabric. 'It's green but it has a fine pink stripe.' He paused for a beat. 'It matches your beautiful eyes. They're green, just like Mum's.'

His words wove magic. Sasha's expression transformed from sceptical to delighted. 'I'll try it on. And these shorts, too.' Sasha took the hanger from her father's hand, grabbed the matching shorts and marched toward the change room.

Laughter bubbled up inside Kate at the exchange between father and daughter. He was good! Wily, but good. Sasha had no idea she'd just been outplayed. Usually dads lost the fashion battles, which was why mothers took on that role.

He turned toward the change rooms and caught her gaze, giving her a conspiratorial grin. 'Let's hope that saves me from a trip to Dubbo.'

Kate forgot to breathe.

Azure eyes flecked with myriad shades of blue sparkled at her, along with a slightly crooked smile. A smile that belonged to a pirate. A smile formed by a mouth that promised all things deliciously wicked.

Where on earth had *that* thought come from?

She gave herself a mental shake. She wasn't shopping for a man. She wasn't even window-shopping. Shane had cured her of every romantic notion she'd ever held.

Besides, this man was a husband and a father. He had a wife with beautiful eyes. Perhaps that's why the errant thought had played across her mind. He was an unavailable man and her radar had relaxed.

She returned his smile. 'I think your days are numbered and it won't be Dubbo she'll be demanding, but the shopping delights of Sydney.'

'You're probably right.' His grin faded, chased away by a shadow that flickered across his face as he shoved his large hands into the pockets of his chinos.

'Dad, what do you think?' Sasha reappeared and did a twirl in her matching outfit, her eyes anxiously seeking his approval.

'You look gorgeous, sweetheart.'

Sasha rolled her eyes. 'You *always* say that, Dad, even when I'm splattered in mud after soccer.'

'Well, you do.' The love in his voice radiated around the shop.

Kate tried to ignore the slug of loss that turned over inside her like a lead weight. What would it be like to be loved like that?

'Um, excuse me, but do you think this colour suits me?' Sasha directed her question to Kate.

Kate took in the tanned, healthy glow of the child, her shiny chestnut hair and large, green eyes. 'Your dad's right. That green does suit you.' A streak of mischief shot through her. 'And you know what would look really great with it? One of those new belts and a matching bracelet and necklace. They've got a rack of accessories to match each outfit.' She pointed toward the display.

Sasha's eyes widened as she caught sight of the trinkets. 'Ooh, and bags, too.'

The pirate groaned and shook his dark head, his thick curls shaking in resignation. 'Thanks for that.'

His sarcasm wasn't lost on Kate and she laughed. 'My pleasure. I'm happy to help. Have fun.' She picked up the same vest top for her niece and walked toward the checkout, a sense of lightness dancing through her. It had been a long time since she'd felt so carefree in Warragurra.

For the first time she realised she was ready to go back to work. At work she'd be surrounded by the security of familiar faces and colleagues who understood. Armed with support like that, of course she could cope with the town.

A shimmer of anxiety skated along her veins, which she promptly squashed. After all, how bad could coming back to Warragurra really be?

'I need to talk to you.' Jen, the office manager of the Warragurra Flying Doctors' Base, called to Baden as he walked briskly past her desk.

'Sorry, Jen. Can't do it now, I'm late. Sasha had an excursion and somewhere between home and school the permission slip vanished. I've just debased myself totally, begging the vice-principal to bend the rules and allow her to go,' Baden Tremont called over his shoulder as he quickly checked the contents of his medical bag.

'I'm sure you charmed her with that smile of yours but I need to talk to you about—'

Baden briskly snapped the clasps of his large black bag closed. 'Email me.' He strode toward the door, knowing he was cutting his departure way too fine.

Jen jogged behind him, trying to keep up. 'I already did but it bounced back as undeliverable and I've had to change—'

'Did you tell Emily? She can fill me in on the plane.' His hand connected with the doorhandle.

'Yes, but...' Jen's words disappeared, captured by the hot wind and drowned out by the engine noise that surged inside when Baden opened the door.

Hell, he really was late. The early morning flight from Broken Hill was touching down. The smell of burning rubber seared his nostrils as he stepped out onto the already steaming tarmac.

Jen continued talking despite the noise. 'Emily…Kate… flight…'

He only caught a few fragments of the words over the din but he had no time to stop. 'Is Emily late?'

Jen shook her head and threw her hands up in frustration.

He gave her a grin, one that usually got him out of trouble, waved and mouthed, 'Tell me at three.'

His last glance was Jen muttering as she stomped back inside.

He hated being late. But the balancing act of full-time doctor and full-time single father meant he was frequently late both professionally and personally. Five months ago when he'd moved to Warragurra from Adelaide, he'd thought the move to the country would give him more time. He'd got that wrong. Remote areas were medically under-resourced.

He took the plane's steps two at a time as a familiar thrill zipped through him. Life might not be how he'd imagined it four years ago but being part of the Flying Doctors' team went a long way toward providing him with professional satisfaction. He'd accepted that was how things had to be. His life offered professional satisfaction. He didn't expect anything more.

The plane door closed behind him and he signalled to Glen Jacobs, the pilot, that he'd checked the lock. 'Morning, Emily.' He caught sight of his flight nurse's legs as she leaned into a storage compartment.

Funny, he'd only ever seen Emily wear long trousers. Somehow he hadn't imagined her legs to be quite so shapely. Or as long. Come to think of it, he'd never imagined anything about Emily. She barely made it to five feet four and her uniform always seemed to hang off her, giving her a shapeless look. The only thing he regularly noticed was how her hair changed colour every third week.

He and Emily had been a team since he'd arrived in

Warragurra. Steady and reliable, she had a no-nonsense approach and got the job done. Home was often chaotic and sadness crept around the edges but Emily made work easy. She was like one of the boys. Happy to talk cricket, tennis and car engines, she was often found at the pub on a Friday night beating anyone brave enough to take her on at the pool table.

He heard her muffled greeting and kept talking, his back to her as he stowed his bag. 'What's Jen in a flap about? I thought she was telling me you were late.'

'I think perhaps she was telling you I was Kate.'

He turned abruptly at the rich and throaty yet vaguely familiar voice.

A tall, willowy woman met his gaze. A startled look crossed her face, racing down to bee-stung lips, which compressed slightly before relaxing into a hint of a smile. Large brown eyes, their gaze serious, blinked against a flash of surprise. 'H-hello.'

He guessed he looked equally astonished. Unexpected warmth spread through him at seeing her again. A type of warmth he hadn't experienced in a long time. 'Hello.' He extended his hand. 'I'm Baden Tremont and you cost me an extra forty-five dollars yesterday.'

This time she smiled a full, wide smile and the serious edge in her eyes softened, changing her look completely. 'A girl lives to accessorise, Doctor, didn't you know that?'

He laughed. 'I'm learning fast.'

She stepped forward with natural grace, taking his hand with a firm grip. 'I'm Kate. Nurse Practitioner.'

Her smooth skin glided softly against his palm and his mind emptied. A tingle of sensation shot through him, stirring his blood for the first time since Annie's death.

Shocking him to his toes.

He abruptly dropped her hand. He covered his rudeness by

indicating they should both sit down. 'Pleased to meet you, Kate.' Had she mentioned a surname? He forced a smile. 'Call me Baden. We should buckle up. Sorry to have kept you waiting. Is Emily sick?'

Kate slid into her seat, crossing her long legs. Baden's gaze followed the movement as if hypnotised.

Stop gawking. He dragged his gaze away and focussed intently on the buckles of the safety harness wondering what the hell was wrong with him.

'I don't think so. She looked her usual hale and hearty self this morning when she flew out to Barcoo Station with Linton.'

Confusion snagged him. 'Linton Gregory? The doctor in charge of A and E at the base hospital?'

She nodded. 'That's right. A couple of times a year he spends two weeks with us. Emily always accompanies him as she has so much experience. It's a good link between the two organisations. Bridge building never goes astray.' Slender fingers expertly snapped the buckles of the harness in place. She tilted her head. 'You're frowning at me—is something wrong?'

He started at the direct question. 'Um, sorry. It's just this has a surreal feeling of being my first day at a new school where everyone else knows each other and how things work. The only problem is that I'm not the new person, you are.'

She laughed. 'I'm not actually new. I've worked for the Flying Doctors for four years. I saw your name on the email that Jen sent out on Friday outlining the changes, so I assumed you were expecting me. Besides, didn't Emily tell you?'

Your email bounced back as undeliverable. Jen had tried to tell him but what about Emily? He racked his brains. 'Come to think of it, on Friday night she did thump me on the back after beating me at pool and said, "Doc, you're a good bloke to work with."'

Kate's mouth broadened into a knowing smile. 'That's Emily's code for saying goodbye.'

A thread of unease vibrated deep inside him. Goodbye? *No.* He wanted to keep working with Emily. Emily was safe and uncomplicated. She didn't stir up sensations he'd forgotten existed. Surely Emily was just spending a couple of weeks with Linton as part of the bridge-building exercise.

Of course, that was it. Just a temporary change.

Once he'd embraced the exhilaration of change. He used to actively seek it out, loving to juggle up the mix. But when Annie had got sick, uncertainty had marched into their life, changing it for ever. Now he craved stability for himself and Sasha. Especially for Sasha.

Of course he could cope for a fortnight working with a tall and slender colleague even if her standard-issue blue blouse seemed to hug her in all the right places. She was a nurse, just like Emily. He swallowed a sigh as he caught sight of her toned calves. He didn't suppose it was PC to suggest she wear trousers rather than shorts.

The engines burst into life, their noise immediately killing the conversation. Baden lifted his green headphones over his ears and adjusted the black mouthpiece so he could hear any last-minute instructions from Glen.

He loved take-off. Loved the roar of the engines, the thrust of power, the torque and the pressure against his chest as acceleration increased and the plane tilted for its fast climb. It gave him an endorphin rush every single time. He forgot his unease and relaxed into the power surge.

The red earth of the outback opened out underneath them, endless red sand bound together by green-grey spinifex. A ute far below sent up a plume of dust into the cloudless blue sky as it travelled along a straight road. Kangaroos bounded with purpose in the cool of the morning. In an hour or so they'd be sheltering in the shade of the gnarled gum trees that clearly marked the winding path of the muddy Darling River, once the transportation lifeline of outback New South Wales.

It took a lot of imagination to picture the 'river jam' of a century ago. One hundred paddle steamers had plied the river, their barges groaning with bales of wool as they'd connected the outback stations with the southern cities. In today's drought, the river was a trickle of its former glory.

He glanced across at Kate. Her eyes sparkled and her face glowed as she peered out the window, her fingers spread against the Perspex. She didn't look like an experienced flight nurse. She looked like a child on her first flight.

She turned away from the window and caught him staring at her. She gave an embarrassed shrug and spoke into her mouthpiece. 'I love the view.'

'It's pretty spectacular if you're not into green, rolling hills.'

She nodded. 'I've been in Europe and although I adored the greenness, I've just realised how much I missed this view. There's a certain rugged beauty about scrubby vegetation and red sand.'

Surprise snagged him. It was like putting together a difficult jigsaw puzzle. Right up to this point he'd thought she was a transfer from another base. 'You've seen this view before?'

'Oh, yes, lots of times.' She picked up a procedures folder as if she was going to read rather than talk.

He tried to ignore the irrational feeling of being overlooked. 'But not recently?'

She shook her head, her chestnut bob caressing her cheeks, highlighting the fine line of her jaw. She seemed to hesitate before speaking. 'I've been away for six months. Today is my first day back.'

Suddenly things started to line up in his brain. He vaguely remembered seeing the name Kate Kennedy on orientation documents when he'd first started. It had caught his attention because the Kennedy name meant money in Warragurra. The family construction company built or renovated just about every substantial public building in the town and had contracts on many of the cattle stations.

That's why she hadn't mentioned her last name when she'd introduced herself—typical Warragurra style. His brief experience with the three prominent families in town had been the same. They all assumed you knew them by the nature of their community standing. 'We must have just missed each other. I started in September last year. So you must be Kate Kennedy?'

Her jaw stiffened slightly, the tremor running down her neck and along her arm. 'My surname is Lawson.' The words snapped out, matching the flash of fire in her eyes. Her body language brooked no argument. It clearly said, Get it right and don't ask why.

He recognised her posture. He'd used it often enough himself to deflect questions. But it was a strong response over a name. Perhaps Lawson was her professional name? A lot of his female colleagues retained their maiden names for work.

He let it slide, wanting to establish some working esprit de corps. 'You must have left just before I arrived in Warragurra. Welcome back, Kate.'

'Thanks.' Her eyes softened. A wistful tone entered her voice. 'I hope it's going to be good.'

'Coming back from a long break is always a bit of an adjustment.' He remembered how tough it had been when he'd returned to work after Annie's death. All those sympathetic faces. He pushed the memory away. 'Still, two weeks working with me will be a good way to ease back into the routine and then you'll be set to take over your usual clinic runs.'

She blinked twice and her smooth brow creased in a fine line. 'This is my usual run.'

His gut tightened, his unease strengthening. 'But Emily—'

'Was filling in for me while I was on leave.'

Her quiet words exploded like a bomb in his brain. *No. No.* He didn't want this. 'So you and I, we're now Flight Team Four?'

'We are.' She smiled again.

Her enthusiastic vibes radiated around him, sparking off a trail of heat that coursed through him, completely disconcerting him. His mind creaked to the inevitable, unwanted conclusion. 'And Emily has been reassigned?'

'She has.'

'Right.' The tightness of his throat strangled the word. *Think.* This wasn't really a problem. He'd just ask for another nurse.

The booming voice of the regional director sounded in his head. *Teamwork is the key. Get your hormones under control and deal with it.*

A shadow floated through Kate's caramel-brown eyes before resignation pushed it aside. She laced her hands in her lap. 'I'm sorry this change of roster caught you by surprise but I'm sure it won't take too long for us to get used to each other.' She gave a throaty laugh. 'After all, I don't bite.'

An image of her lush, red lips and her white teeth nibbling his neck slammed into him.

This wasn't happening. He didn't react like this to women. He couldn't. For years he'd seen women as colleagues, employees, sisters, mothers, friends. He packaged women into neat, safe boxes.

And that was exactly what he had to do now. Find a box for

Kate. She would go into the workbox. And it would be a very secure, firm box with a lid that would not open.

He could do that. Of course he could do that.

How hard could it be?

CHAPTER TWO

KATE twisted open the top of a bottle of ice-cold water and drank half of the contents in one go. After recapping the bottle, she ran it across the back of her neck, savouring the coolness against her hot skin. She glanced out toward the endless burnt brown paddocks and beyond to the horizon which blurred with shimmering heat. Cattle clustered under the few available scrubby trees, seeking shade in the midday heat.

Coming out of a European winter and straight back into a Warragurra summer was like crashing into a brick wall, except the wall was all-encompassing, energy-draining heat. She must be mad. She should have delayed her return and spent two more months in France and Italy. But Warragurra was home. At least it had been, and she planned to make it home again no matter what anyone else thought.

'Hot one for you today, Kate.' Barry Sanderson, the taciturn owner of Camoora Station, lifted his hat and ran his forearm across his sweaty brow.

Kate smiled. She'd missed the ironic understatement of the Australian outback. It was *always* hot in February in western New South Wales. 'It's a stinker. Thanks for giving me the shadiest spot on the veranda for my baby clinic.'

'You know for as long as Mary and I are here, you're *always* welcome at Camoora.' Understanding crossed his weatherworn face before his voice became gruff, as if he'd exposed too much of his feelings. 'Besides, we can't have those babies overheated.'

'Thanks, Barry.' She continued swiftly, not wanting to embarrass him but grateful for his support. 'I'd better get back to work. Can't have the new doc beating me on my first day back.'

Barry put his hat back on his head. 'You make sure you have some tea and scones with Mary sooner rather than later.' He strode down the long veranda of the homestead, stopping to talk to Baden.

Kate watched the interchange—the stocky bushman and the tall, athletic doctor. Baden was as dark as Barry was fair. She'd been stunned this morning when he'd turned around and faced her on the plane. Yesterday's pirate was a doctor.

A disconcerted doctor. He'd looked almost worried when he'd realised the two of them were now Team Four. That had thrown her. She was used to all sorts of expressions from half the town— disdain, hatred and loathing. But work was different. At work she was valued, admired, respected. Or at least she had been.

Teamwork was the basis of the Flying Doctors. The working day meant a lot of time was spent with your team colleague. She'd hoped to resume working with Doug Johnston, but he'd transferred to Muttawindi two months ago covering Bronte Morrison's maternity leave. He wouldn't be back in Warragurra for a year.

We must have just missed each other. I started in September last year. Her stomach dropped as she recalled Baden's words. He and his family would have arrived in Warragurra just as the Kennedys had finally realised they had no legal standing to contest Shane's will. Just as the vitriol in the local press had reached its zenith. In many circles in the town her name was mud. Perhaps Baden's wife had heard the rumours and not heard the truth.

Tension tugged at her temples with a vice-like grip. Work was her sanctuary while she found her feet again in the town. She must make this assignment with Baden work. Only her actions could dissolve rumours and innuendo. She had to prove to him she was a professional who could be relied on, a team player. Someone he could depend on as much as he'd obviously depended on Emily.

She watched him walk along the veranda toward her, his moleskins moving against his thighs, outlining hard muscle. 'Ah, the baby clinic.' He rubbed his hands together. 'It's one of my favourites.' His smile raced across his face, lighting his eyes, making them sparkle with anticipation.

His smile sent her blood racing to her feet, making her feel light-headed. 'I know what you mean. A roly-poly baby, healthy on breast milk reaffirms that life is good.'

They quickly established a pattern of weighing and measuring babies, reassuring anxious mothers and immunizing babies against childhood illnesses. Kate dealt with any breast-feeding issues and Baden examined the babies with reflux.

With companionable teamwork and a lot of laughter they tested the hearing of all the eight-month-old babies. Baden entertained each mother and baby with his Peter the Penguin puppet, while Kate shook the rattle behind the baby's ears.

Baden's experience as a father came through as he managed to relax the mums and the babies with the antics of the hand puppet. Kate imagined he would have read great stories to Sasha, complete with a cast of voices for the characters.

In the distance a child's scream rent the air as Kate called her next mother and baby.

'Looks like we might be patching yet another knee and dispensing a lollypop,' Baden commented as he filled in an immunisation record.

Kate nodded. 'I think that will be number six for the day. Gravel paths and toddlers don't really mix.' She turned and called her next patient. 'So, Ginny, how's baby Samantha going?'

Ginny cuddled the baby in close. 'Pretty well, although I think she's been having a growth spurt as she's been feeding a lot.'

Kate checked Samantha's date of birth. 'Well, at six weeks you'd expect—'

'Help me! Will someone help me?' A woman's frantic voice carried across the yard, her distress palpable.

'Sorry, Ginny.' Kate spun around, reaching for the emergency kit, her hand colliding with Baden's.

He grasped the handle. 'I've got it. Follow me.'

He ran down the veranda as Mary Sanderson came into view, carrying her four-year-old daughter. Her eldest daughter, Kelly, ran close behind.

Blood covered the little girl's face as she lay whimpering in her mother's arms. 'What happened?' Baden gently guided the woman into a scat.

'She was feeding the chooks with her big sister, like she does every afternoon. Kelly said she heard Susie scream and she turned around to find the rooster had knocked her flat. I can't believe a rooster could knock a child over.' Incredulity marked her face. 'I've spent all my life on a farm and I've never seen that happen.'

Kelly bit her lip. 'The rooster was on Susie's chest and pecking her and I ran at it but it wouldn't let go. I threw the bucket at it but while I was picking her up it flew at her again.' She gave a quiet sob. 'It was really scary.'

Kate squeezed Kelly's shoulder. 'You did a great job, Kelly. Dr Baden and I will soon have the blood cleaned up and it won't look so scary.' She opened up normal saline and began to clean Susie's face with gauze so they could clearly see the extent of the damage.

Susie's petrified screams pulled at her. The little girl's face seemed to be swelling under Kate's fingers as she wiped the blood away. Her puffy eyes were slits in her face and her cheeks were increasing in size.

Baden's long fingers gently sought a pulse in the wriggling child's neck, which he counted against the second hand of his watch. 'Susie, I'm just going to listen to your chest with my stethoscope.' He bent down so he was at the same level as the little girl and showed her the round end that would lie against her chest.

Susie's crying halted for a moment but then she started to cough—probably induced by the hysterical screaming. The coughing eased and she lay exhausted in her mother's arms.

Apprehension skated through Kate as her trauma radar tuned in. Something wasn't quite right. Superficial lacerations didn't usually cause swelling like this. As she grabbed more gauze she caught Baden's worried expression.

He felt it, too—the aura of disquiet seemed to blanket them both.

She quickly and deftly used the gauze to clean away the large amount of blood on the child's neck. Blood oozed out as fast as she could clear it. 'Baden.' She hoped he could decode the tone of her voice.

He immediately pulled the earpiece out of his ear, his concentration firmly on her. 'Yes?'

'There's a really deep wound on her throat and her neck is swelling fast. I'm worried about her airway.'

'So am I. Her air entry is diminished.'

'What do you mean?' Mary's voice wobbled. 'It's just a few scratches, isn't it?'

Baden carefully examined Susie's throat, his fingers gently palpating around the base of her throat. 'There's air under her skin.'

'Air? That can't be good.' Kate reached for the walkie-talkie.

He rubbed the back of his neck. 'It's subcutaneous emphysema. I think the rooster has perforated her trachea—the tube that takes the air to the lungs—and now air is escaping into the skin.'

Mary's hand flew to her own throat. 'Can she breathe?'

'She's breathing on her own at the moment but the risk is that the bleeding and swelling will block the tube. We're going to have to get her stable and then evacuate her to hospital.'

Kate immediately called Glen on the walkie-talkie. 'We need the stretcher, Glen. Susie Sanderson needs oxygen and evacuation, over.'

'On my way, over.' Glen's voice crackled into the dry, hot air.

Mary, her eyes wide with fear, looked frantically at them both as Baden's words finally sank in. 'She'll go to Warragurra Hospital, won't she?'

'No, I'm sorry but she needs to go to the Women's and Children's Hospital in Adelaide.' He rested his hand on Mary's for a brief moment. 'I'm going to need to examine her fully.'

'Glen's on his way with the stretcher, which will double as a treatment bed.' Kate pulled out the paediatric oxygen mask and unravelled the green tubing, making it all ready to connect the moment the stretcher and oxygen arrived.

'Give us a hand, Kate.'

Glen's voice hailed her from the bottom of the stairs. She quickly ran to meet him and helped to lift the stretcher up onto the veranda.

Baden's strong arms gently transferred Susie onto the stretcher, sitting her up to aid her laboured breathing. 'Kate's going to put a mask on you to help you feel better and Mummy's here to hold your hand.'

His tenderness with Susie touched Kate. Not all doctors were at ease with kids. But he was a father and had probably spent a few nights walking the floor.

'I want a drink,' Susie sobbed between fits of jagged crying.

Kate adjusted the clear mask to Susie's face, making sure it was a snug fit by pulling on the green elastic. 'I'm sorry, sweetie, you can't have a drink but I'm going to give you a drink in your arm.' Kate checked with Baden. 'Normal saline IV?'

He nodded, a flash of approval in his eyes. 'Yes, saline. You all right to insert it?' He paused for a moment in his examination of Susie's back.

For a brief moment she was tempted to say no. She'd been out of the field for six months and Shane's parents' campaign against her had dented her confidence. But she had to show Baden she was a team player and totally reliable. 'Sure, no problem.'

You've done this hundreds of times. Don't let the Kennedys invade work.

'Susie, this will sting just a little bit, OK? You squeeze Mummy's hand really tight.' She adjusted the tourniquet and palpated for a vein. Her fingers detected a small rise and she swabbed the little girl's arm, the alcohol stinging her nostrils.

'OK, here we go.' Carefully she slid the intravenous cannula into the vein, controlling the pressure so there was enough to pierce the skin but not too much that she put the needle through the vein.

'Mummy, stop her,' Susie squealed as the needle penetrated the skin.

Kate bit her lip. 'Nearly there, Susie.' Holding her breath, she withdrew the trocar. Blood.

Yes. She released her breath and taped the needle in place. 'IV inserted, Baden.'

He gave her a wide smile of acknowledgment—a smile that raced to his vivid blue eyes and caused them to crinkle at the edges.

A smile that melted something inside her and sent spirals of molten warmth through her, reaching all the way down to her toes.

Stop it. Thank goodness he was married and off limits. Otherwise that smile could batter all her resolutions about staying single. She found her voice. 'Do you want a bolus of three hundred millilitres?'

'Yes, good idea. I'm worried about bleeding.'

'What about pain relief?' It was a tricky situation.

'Morphine would be good for the pain so she would be more comfortable and start to breathe more easily, but it also depresses the respiratory system. It's catch-22.' He frowned and rubbed the back of his neck, the same action he'd used when he'd told Mary about the perforated trachea. 'We'll titrate it in through the IV and that way we can control it and pull it if we need to.'

'Mary?' Kate got her attention. 'How much does Susie weigh? I need as accurate a weight as possible.'

The distraught mother spoke slowly. 'I… It's been a while since I weighed her but she'd be about twenty kilograms, I think.'

'Baden?' He'd lifted her onto the stretcher.

He nodded. 'That's about right.' He gave Susie's knee a rub. 'You weigh the same as the sacks of flour I buy to make bread.'

Susie gave a wan smile.

Kate calculated the dose. 'So two milligrams of morphine.'

'Correct.' Baden checked the dose with her as mandated by the Dangerous Drug Act.

He called to Glen. 'We need to go.' He rested his hand on Mary's shoulder. 'Are you or Barry coming with us or will you follow on your own?'

'Mary's going with Susie.' Barry's gruff voice cracked on the words. 'I'm going to go and kill that bloody rooster.'

'After you've done that, pack them both a case, Barry, and we'll radio you when we get back to Warragurra.' Kate hugged the usually stoic man and ran down the steps.

Kate gave thanks that the airstrip at Camoora Station was very close to the homestead. Station hands, their dusty faces lined with anxiety, carried the stretcher as if it were porcelain, avoiding jolting the adored Susie, hoping their care would help.

Seven minutes after Baden had issued the order to depart, the PC-12 aircraft was racing down the dusty runway.

Kate did the first set of in-flight observations. Susie's heart was racing and her breathing rapid and shallow. 'She's tachycardic and tachypnoeic,' she informed Baden sotto voce the moment he signed off from the radio conversation with the paediatric registrar in Adelaide.

He placed his stethoscope on Susie's back and listened intently. 'Nothing is getting into the lower lobe of her left lung.' Deep furrows scored his forehead as he leant across her to check the IV.

The fragrance of spicy aftershave mixing with his masculine scent filled Kate's nostrils and she wanted to breathe in deeply. Instead, she deliberately leaned back and concentrated on filling in the fluid balance chart. 'Are you thinking pneumothorax?'

'I'm certain the lower lobe of her lung has collapsed but at the moment her body's compensating. I'm not rushing into a needle thoracentesis without X-ray guidance unless I have to.' He shook his head in disbelief. 'It was such a brutal attack. I can't believe a rooster's beak could cause such damage.'

'It wouldn't have been the beak. It was the spur on the foot. They're viciously sharp.'

He raised his brows. 'You seem to know a bit about poultry.'

She shrugged. 'Born and raised a country girl. What about you?'

'City boy. Grew up on the Adelaide beaches.'

She laughed. 'Linton would say that Adelaide and city was an oxymoron.'

Baden raised his brows. 'From Sydney, is he?' He chuckled. 'I'll have you know that peak hour lasts half an hour.'

His rich laugh relaxed her. 'Peak hour in Warragurra is Saturday night when the station hands drive into town. Even from Adelaide it's a big leap.' She checked Susie's pulse. 'What brought you here?'

'It was something I'd talked about doing for a long time.' He had a far-away look in his eyes as if he was recalling memories.

She jotted down the volume of the new bag of IV fluid that she had just attached to Susie's drip. 'And suddenly the time seemed right?'

His relaxed demeanour instantly vanished. 'Something like that.' His voice developed an edge to it, a tone she'd not heard before.

Before she could wonder too much about what that might mean, Susie started coughing. Kate immediately aspirated her mouth but the child continued to gasp, her lips turning blue.

'She's obstructing!' She snapped opened the laryngoscope, the tiny light bulb glowing white. 'Intubation?'

'What's happening?' Mary's petrified voice sounded from her seat at the front of the plane.

'We have to put a tube in Susie's throat so she can breathe.' Kate wanted to go and hug the distraught mother but all her attention was needed for Susie.

Mary's gasp of horror echoed around the plane.

Baden accepted the laryngoscope, a grim expression on his face. 'I doubt I'll be able to pass the tube through the swelling.' He tried inserting the 'scope but a moment later shook his head. 'No go.'

Kate's stomach dropped and she swung into emergency

action. 'Right, then. Tracheostomy it is.' She opened the paediatric emergency cricothyroidotomy kit, which she'd had ready since they'd boarded the flight.

Susie's small chest struggled to rise and fall, each breath more torturous than the last.

Baden snapped on gloves and grabbed the scalpel.

A sharp incessant beeping from the monitor hammered the air as Susie's oxygen saturation levels started to fall to dangerously low levels. Each beep told them Susie was edging closer to cardiac arrest.

'Save my daughter, please!'

Mary's tortured plea ripped through Kate. She quickly laid the semi-conscious child on her back and extended her neck.

Baden threw her a look, his eyes dark with worry. This procedure on a child was fraught with danger but they had no choice. With a remarkably steady hand he gently palpated Susie's neck, counting down the rings of cartilage until he found the correct position. He made a quick, clean cut.

Kate immediately cleared the area of blood with a gauze pad. She pulled the sterile packaging of the endotracheal tube halfway down, exposing the top of the tube and insertion trocar.

Baden juggled the forceps and then grabbed the tube, sliding it into place.

Kate swiftly attached the oxygen. A moment later the monitor stopped screaming as Susie's oxygen level rose. A sigh shuddered out of Kate's lungs as she injected normal saline into the balloon of the ET tube to hold it in place.

Baden raised his head from his patient and turned toward Mary. 'We've bypassed the blockage and she's breathing more easily now.'

Mary slumped. 'Oh, thank you, Baden. Kate. I was so scared that she might…'

Baden nodded. 'She'll probably have to go to Theatre when we arrive in Adelaide to repair her lung and trachea, and when the swelling has subsided, this tube can come out.'

He turned back to Kate and spoke under his breath. 'So much for a quiet first day back at work for you. Nothing like an emergency to pump the adrenaline around.' He stripped off his gloves. 'Thanks, Kate. That was excellent work.' His lips curved upward in a friendly smile. 'It's good to have you on board.'

'Thanks. It's good to be back.' Delicious, simmering warmth rolled through her, quickly overtaken by sheer relief. She'd managed to drive away his doubts, the ones that had shone so brightly that morning in his amazing eyes.

Her plan had worked. She'd shown him she knew what she was about, that her medicine was sound. She'd managed to stay one stop ahead of him during the emergency and at times their anticipation of each other's needs had been almost spooky.

For the first time all day she relaxed. Team Four would be OK. Work would again be the safe sanctuary it had always been—reliable and familiar. No surprises.

Smiling to herself, she adjusted Susie's oxygen and started to dress her lacerations with non-stick gauze.

'Prepare for landing.' Glen's command sounded in her ears and with one final check of Susie she took her seat, snapping her harness firmly around her.

The paediatric team met them at the airport in Adelaide and within minutes Susie and Mary were on their way to hospital and the ICU unit.

As always happened after a high-powered emergency, Kate's legs began to wobble. Coffee. She needed coffee. The refrigerated air of the airport terminal hit her the moment she stepped inside. She ordered three coffees to go and some giant cookies so heavily laden with chocolate chips you could hardly see the actual cookie base. Juggling the capped coffees and her bag of treats, she headed back toward the plane. Glen usually liked to get back in the air as soon as possible.

As she approached she saw Baden striding back and forth across the tarmac, his mobile phone glued to his ear and his other hand rubbing his neck. Agitation rolled off him in waves—a total contrast to the cool and level-headed doctor she'd just worked with in an emergency.

He snapped the phone shut just as she stopped beside him. She passed him his coffee.

'Oh, thanks.' He accepted the coffee with a distracted air.

'Let's move under the wing—at least there's shade there.' She offered him a cookie as they took the five steps into the shadow of the plane. 'Is there a problem?'

He blew out a breath. 'Sasha is refusing to go to after-school care. She's never done this before, she's always been happy to go. I don't know why she had to pull this stunt today, the one day in weeks I've been delayed.'

Confusion befuddled her brain. 'Why is the school ringing *you*?'

He shot her a look of incredulity that screamed she was an imbecile. 'Because I'm her father!'

His frustration hit her in the chest like a ball on the full, almost making her stagger. Rattled, she chose her words carefully. 'Yes, I understand that, but you're in Adelaide and your wife's in Warragurra. Surely she can get away from work for half an hour to talk to Sasha?'

His hand tightened on the cookie, sending crumbs tumbling toward the ground. 'I don't have a wife. It's just Sasha and me.' His phone rang loudly and he spun away to answer it.

I don't have a wife. He'd spoken the words softly but they boomed in Kate's head as if she were standing in front of a

500-watt concert speaker. The five small words tangled in her brain like knotted fishing wire, refusing to straighten out and make sense.

He was a single parent.

Questions surged through her, desperate for answers, but Baden had his back to her, his entire being focussed on the phone call.

She watched him end his call and consult with Glen, his dark curly hair, flecked with grey, moving in the wind. Then he tilted his head back, downing his coffee in two gulps, his Adam's apple moving convulsively against his taut neck. Crushing the empty cup in his strong hand, he swung around, his free arm beckoning her forward.

As she drew up beside him he stood back to allow her entry to the plane's steps. 'Glen's ready to leave, so after you…' His eyes sparkled as he gave her a resigned smile. A Pirate smile. Delicious and dangerous.

Her blood rushed to her feet as realisation hit her. *He's not married.* Together they were Team Four. They had to work side by side every day. The attraction she'd easily shrugged off yesterday and earlier today suddenly surged through her like water through a narrow gorge—powerful and strong.

The safe sanctuary that was work, the sanctuary she so desperately needed, vaporised before her eyes.

Baden stacked the dishwasher, his thoughts not on the china but on trying to come up with the best approach to handle Sasha's rebellion. She'd made herself scarce, knowing he wasn't thrilled with her behaviour. He could see her out the window, jumping on the trampoline, her long brown hair streaming out behind her.

It's chestnut, like Kate's. The unexpected thought thudded into him, startling him.

Kate had worked alongside him today as if she'd done it every day for a year. Calm, experienced and knowledgeable, she got the job done. Just like Emily. Except Emily didn't wear a perfume that conjured up hot tropical nights and sinful pleasures.

He slammed the dishwasher closed. What was he doing, thinking of Kate, when his concentration should be firmly on Sasha? Guilt niggled at him. He'd promised Annie that Sasha would always be his top priority. Hell, it was no hardship. He adored his daughter. But he missed sharing the parenting journey.

Sasha had finished on the trampoline and was lying in the hammock, which was permanently slung between two veranda posts. It had been a much-adored Christmas present and had saved him from buying the requested pink mobile phone, which he planned to put off for as long as possible.

He pushed the fly-wire screen door open and walked toward her. 'I thought you might like an ice cream.'

Sasha looked up and swung her legs over the side of the hammock, taking the proffered confectionary. 'Cool. I didn't know we had any of these left.'

'I went shopping.' He sat down next to her, his weight sending the hammock swinging wildly, causing Sasha to fall onto him.

'Da-ad,' she rebuked him, but stayed snuggled up next to him, the back of her head resting on his chest. Ice cream dribbled down her chin.

His heart lurched. In so many ways she was still his little girl, but for how long? The signs of impending puberty were beginning to shout. 'Sash, why did you give Mrs Davidson such a hard time this afternoon?'

She licked her ice cream. 'I didn't want to go to after-school care.'

'That bit I understand. It's why you didn't want to go that's bothering me.'

'It's for babies.' A belligerent tone crept into her voice.

He breathed in and focussed on keeping his words neutral and even. 'It's for all kids from prep to grade six.'

'But I'm twelve and can look after myself after school.'

He gave an internal sigh. 'We've had this discussion before, Sash, and because work is sometimes unpredictable and I occasionally have to transport patients to Broken Hill, Dubbo or Adelaide, I need to know that you're safe.'

'But I'd be safe here.' She turned, her earnest green eyes imploring him to understand. 'Besides, Erin isn't going any more. Her mum stopped working and she's getting to do cool stuff, like going to Guides on Wednesdays and swimming on Fridays.'

He ran his hand through his hair. Erin Baxter and Sasha were inseparable friends. Without Erin's company, after-school care would seem like jail. All the other children who attended were in the junior classes at the school. 'Why didn't you tell me Erin wasn't there?'

She shrugged. 'You would have said I still had to go and I hate it without her. There's no one to hang out with. I wish that…I wish I could just come home after school.'

Her unspoken words hovered around them both, pulling at him, twisting his guilt. Before Annie's death Sasha had always been able to come home straight after school.

'I'm sorry I'm not here after school and I'm sorry Mum's not here.' He hugged her tight. 'What if I talk to Erin's mum and ask if she would mind taking you to swimming, too? I have Wednesday afternoons in the office so if we find out what time Guides is on, perhaps I can take you. That only leaves three days of after-school care. Deal?'

Her eyes danced with joy. 'Deal. Thanks, Dad.'

He swung his legs into the hammock and lay down next to her. 'You're welcome, sweetheart.' Another crisis solved. Work was uncomplicated and straightforward compared to this parenting gig.

Sasha cuddled in closer now her ice cream was finished. 'Did Emily have purple hair today?' She'd always been impressed by Emily's extremely short rainbow-coloured hair.

He stretched out, enjoying the companionable time with his daughter. 'Actually, Emily isn't working with me at the moment. Do you remember that lady we met when we were buying your new green top? Well, it turns out she's my flight nurse now.'

'Awesome. She had the best smile and a gorgeous skirt.' Sasha propped herself up with one elbow resting on his chest. Her serious gaze searched his face. 'What's she like?'

'She's very good at her job.'

'Yeah, but do you *like* her?' Hope crossed her face.

Unlike adults, kids always cut to the chase, but even so Sasha's unexpected wishful look, combined with the question hit him hard in the chest. To a twelve-year-old, *like* was serious stuff.

Did he *like* Kate? The image of luminous brown eyes, as warm as melted chocolate, filled his head. A streak of unexpected longing shot through him.

Disloyalty followed closely, jagged and sharp.

He sat up abruptly, setting the hammock swinging wildly. He wasn't up to discussing this with Sasha when his reaction to Kate confused the hell out of him. He rolled out of the hammock and stretched his arms down for her. 'Time for bed.'

'Da-ad.'

He hauled her out of the hammock. 'Come on, hop it. Clean your teeth and get into bed. Otherwise you'll never get *Anne of Green Gables* finished.'

The promise of reading time had Sasha dashing for the door, her question about Kate forgotten.

A long breath shuddered out of his lungs. If only he could find Kate that easy to forget.

CHAPTER THREE

'So is everyone clear on the rosters?' Jen's right hand rested firmly on her hip as she looked expectantly at the staff. 'Team Four, your roster has changed a lot so you *must* make sure you have the most up-to-date version.' She narrowed her gaze at Baden. 'The email system is back online and I expect you to check it.' Jen ran a tight ship, holding together a staff of twenty strong personalities.

Everyone nodded and those brave enough even mumbled, 'Yes, Jen.'

'Right, then, thanks for your attention.' Jen tapped a pile of brightly coloured files. 'Please collect a folder on the way out.'

Baden winked at Kate. 'We'd better check our emails.'

'I think that line was directed solely at you. I've still got brownie points up my sleeve.' She couldn't resist teasing him. 'After all, it wasn't me who drove out to Opal Ridge for a clinic on the wrong day.'

A sheepish grin crossed his face. 'Lucky for me old Hughie chose that day to have a hypo so it wasn't a complete waste of time. Now he's completely up to speed with his new glucometer.' He faked a serious expression, the corners of his eyes crinkling with humour. 'Patient education is a very important part of our work, Sister Lawson.'

Laughter rolled through her at his self-deprecating humour, bringing a joy that had faded from her life. 'Is that right, Doctor? I had no idea.'

His laughter joined hers and quickly raced to his eyes, which sparkled like sunshine on water. His work-issue blue shirt intensified the vivid blue of his eyes and enhanced his tanned face. Not to mention the way his chest filled the shirt, making the fabric sit flat against what she imagined was solid muscle.

Her stomach flipped as heat rolled thorough her. *Stop it now.* She crossed her legs, trying to halt the tingling sensations that built up inside her.

It was too depressing to be twenty-nine and reacting like a sixteen-year-old. She was too old for a hormone crush. Too world-weary to have stars in her eyes and too bruised to ever think romance was for her. But her body wasn't listening.

It didn't seem to matter that she'd spoken sternly to herself, that she'd instructed her body *not* to react and that she'd willed herself to be impervious to eyes that sparkled with every shade of blue. It took one smile and her body quivered in anticipation.

She stood up and joined the queue behind Linton and Emily to collect the folder as instructed.

'So, Doc, you thought you'd do a spot of opal fossicking the other day.' Emily immediately teased Baden about his mistake.

'Yeah, and I found one this big.' He held his hands a shoulder width apart. 'But it got away when Hughie hypo'd.'

Kate let the laughter and camaraderie wash over her, savouring it. Wednesday afternoon meant staff meeting. All the teams were back in the office after morning clinics to attend. They took it in turns being the standby emergency team, but it wasn't very often that there was a Wednesday afternoon emergency. It was almost as if the locals knew not to get sick after 1:00 p.m.

If they did get a callout it was usually from tourists who'd got themselves into a spot of bother.

With the exception of the staff meeting, Wednesday was pretty much a Baden-free day. Kate ran an early well-women's clinic in the morning before returning to base for the afternoon.

It had been a relief to work on her own this morning, giving her over-developed radar of Baden a rest. It wasn't that she didn't enjoy working with him. She did. She'd loved her first two days with him. He was on the ball medically, good-humoured most of the time, and he related really well to the patients. But this overwhelming attraction that whizzed through her whenever she was near him was wearing her out.

It was crazy stuff. He was her colleague. She should be noticing how thorough he was with the patients, learning from him as he passed on clinical skills, taking advantage of the way he treated her as an equal, seeking her opinion in tricky cases. And on one level she was doing all those things.

But on another level she was very aware of the way he twirled his pen when he was thinking. How strands of silver hair caressed his temples in stark contrast to the rest of his raven curls, and how his deep, rich laugh was as smooth and velvety as a cellared shiraz.

And she kept wondering how he'd come to be a single father. Where was Sasha's mother?

Was he divorced? Perhaps they'd never married. All the different permutations and combinations ran through her head. Baden hadn't volunteered any more information and the opportunity to ask more direct questions hadn't arisen. She supposed she could ask Emily but it seemed a bit tacky, almost like prying. She'd been on the other end of that. Her life had been pried into, opened up and peeled back like a sardine can. She didn't intend to inflict that invasion of privacy on anyone.

'Are you coming for coffee, Kate?' Linton paused by the door. The 'cappuccino club' met straight after the staff meeting each week. 'We've got Florentines.' His expression of delight made him look like a kid who had just discovered Mum had filled the cookie jar.

She glanced at her watch. Four o'clock—the meeting had run late. Wednesday evening was Guides. She'd been a Guide leader for a couple of years and tonight was her second night back after her break.

She didn't want to be late, especially as one of the Guides had asked if she could bring a friend. That was great as the pack could do with more members. The Kennedy clan had pressured some families to withdraw their daughters and some had capitulated. Others had stayed, although they refused to help out, but she was sticking with it. There were three supportive parents and now she was back she planned to rebuild. Guides would be so much fun that the girls of Warragurra would be begging their parents to attend and to get involved. 'Sorry, I'll have to pass this week. Save me a Florentine.'

Linton nodded and disappeared down the hall with Emily.

She picked up her folder and handed one to Baden. 'Aren't you going for coffee either?'

Baden shook his head. 'I promised Sasha no after-school care on Wednesdays.'

She smiled. 'Negotiated a midweek deal, did you, to sweeten the rest of the week?'

Surprise rippled across his face. 'Something like that. I guess I have to accept she's growing up and perhaps growing out of after-school care, but she's not grown up enough to be on her own.'

Kate nodded slowly, understanding his dilemma. 'It's a tricky age. School holidays must be really tough for you.' *What about Sasha's mother?* She bit off the specific question that gnawed at her. 'Can extended family help you?'

'My parents visit in the holidays.' The words came out curtly, as if they were meant to discourage a response.

He did that occasionally—lurched from extremely friendly to completely closed down whenever the conversation turned to personal things. A few times she'd been on the point of asking if Sasha might like to join Guides, but he always swung the conversation back to work and kept it firmly centred on the job.

Except when he told you he wasn't married.

She thought back to Monday when they'd been in Adelaide. He'd closed down then when he'd told her that, just like he'd closed down now. For whatever reason, he didn't want to talk about Sasha's mother. Perhaps his relationship with her had been as disastrous as hers had with Shane. If it had been, she could totally understand why he avoided the topic. But that didn't help her rampant curiosity. She hated the fact she wanted to know about this woman and the more he deflected the topic, the more she wanted to know.

He walked to the door, pushing it open for her. She ducked under his arm, her shoulder brushing against him. Tingling pleasure pulsated through her, the sensations intensifying as they dived deeper and unfurled like ribbons in the breeze. Her body's reaction to an inadvertent touch was way out of proportion and she tried to shrug the sensations away. Finally, the tingling receded, leaving her bewildered and unsettled.

As they walked down the corridor she concentrated on work, trying to ignore the maelstrom of emotions churning inside her. 'Have you heard from the Women's and Children's in Adelaide?'

He nodded. 'Susie's doing well. She's out of ICU and will probably be transferred to Warragurra tomorrow.'

'Thank goodness. Mary and Barry will be so relieved.'

'Yes, it was a good outcome.' He paused outside his office. 'See you tomorrow, then.'

'Yes, see you tomorrow. 'Night.' She moved toward the door. Thank goodness she could leave the office now. She didn't have to face working with Baden until tomorrow morning. And all her attention for the next few hours would be on the Guides, which would completely block any errant thoughts of a tall, curly-haired doctor.

An hour later she'd negotiated the supermarket, bought a giant container of maple syrup, set up three trestle tables and plugged in a couple of electric frypans. She crossed her fingers that the old hall's fusebox would cope with the power drain.

She checked her watch. Sandra, her assistant, was usually here by now.

The Guides started arriving and she gave them setting-up tasks, keeping them busy.

'Hi, Kate, Mum's sent some eggs from the farm.' Phoebe Walton put a dozen eggs on the trestle table. 'She says you have to take any leftover eggs home.'

'Thanks, Phoebe. Can you head into the kitchen and help Hannah and Jessica in their quest for cooking utensils?'

'Sure.' Phoebe headed to the kitchen.

'I remembered the lemons!' Erin Baxter proudly held a bag of lemons aloft.

'Sensational effort, Erin.' Kate looked beyond her. 'Where's your friend?'

Erin dumped the lemons down hard, sending three rolling down the hall. 'She's coming but Mum couldn't bring her because I had a dentist appointment.' She grimaced.

'I think the fluoro pink brackets look fabulous on your braces.' Kate's mobile phone vibrated in her pocket. 'Excuse me.' She pulled out the phone, immediately recognising the number on the display. 'Hi, Sandra.'

'Joel has just vomited everywhere for the second time and I really can't leave him. Sorry, Kate. Perhaps one of the mothers can stay and help you out?' Sandra's hopeful voice sounded down the line.

Kate didn't have the heart to tell her that the mothers who might have stayed and helped had departed, and by the time she was able to get one of them to come back they would have lost too much time for the session to take place. 'I hope Joel feels better soon.' She rang off.

Hilary Smithton walked in with her daughter, Lucy, her nose wrinkling as if the air of the Guide Hall was offensive. Hilary always arrived late, although Kate doubted it was from disorganisation. Hilary had grown up with Shane. Along with the Kennedy clan, she blamed Kate for his death.

Kate took in a deep breath. 'Hello, Hilary. Hi, Lucy. Did you remember the sugar for the pancakes?'

Lucy cast a worried look at her mother and then stared at the floor.

Hilary put her palm against her chest in an exaggerated movement, her red nails vivid against the white designer T-shirt. 'Oh, dear, were we supposed to bring sugar?'

Kate forced a polite smile. She'd bet her bottom dollar Lucy had asked for the sugar. 'Not to worry, Lucy. I brought some in just in case.'

Relief flooded the girl's face as she ran off to join her patrol.

Kate did a head count. She had more girls than she could legally have in her care alone. She didn't want to have to disappoint them and cancel. Swallowing hard, she smiled at Hilary. 'Sandra Dodson has a sick child and isn't able to assist tonight. Are you able to stay and help out?'

Hilary's gaze swept the hall, taking in the smiling, chattering girls all lined up in their patrols with the expectation of a fun time ahead shining on their faces.

Kate could almost hear Hilary's brain ticking over, working out that without help Guides would have to be cancelled. She gave it one last shot, planning to appeal to Hilary's maternal side. 'Lucy's been so looking forward to earning her cooking badge. Tonight's the final task. It would be disappointing if it couldn't happen.'

Hilary exhaled on a hiss, her eyes narrowing to glinting slits. 'Disappointment is part of life. The sooner she learns that, the better. You might have been able to manipulate Shane but you can't manipulate me.'

For a moment her attention seemed to slide away, as if she was looking over Kate's shoulder. Then her gaze snapped back. 'I refuse to help you, just like you refused to help Shane. And if you run the group tonight without another adult present, I'll report you.'

Kate's fingers curled into fists, her nails digging into her palms. She welcomed the pain as she forced herself to stay calm. She knew Hilary disliked her but she hadn't believed she would jeopardise the Guides.

Anger and frustration welled up inside her. Her first attempt at resuming her life back in Warragurra and she'd failed. Hilary had her neatly over a barrel. How hard did it have to be to live in this town?

'I can stay and help.'

The deep resonance of the words washed over her, causing her breath to catch in her throat. She'd recognise that voice anywhere. She spun around so quickly she swayed.

Baden stood in the hall with Sasha, his expression congenial but his eyes unusually dark, with swirling puzzlement in their depths.

Then he smiled. 'Hello.'

Kate's knees wobbled and she locked them for support. Her heart had already been hammering from the adrenaline surge Hilary's words had evoked. Now his smile added a crazy jumping third beat. It left her dizzy and disorientated.

'Hello, Baden.' She focussed hard to sound cool and in control.

'Erin Baxter invited Sasha to Guides.' The informative statement filled in the gaps, as if he sensed her confusion at seeing him out of context. 'She's been talking about Guides for days so it would be a shame if pancake night couldn't happen.' He shot a wide smile at Hilary. 'Besides, I'm a bit of a pancake expert.'

Hilary stiffened. 'Well, I'll leave you to it, then, Doctor. Although a man present at Guides is not exactly what the organisation had in mind.' She gripped her shoulder-bag close to her side and strode out of the hall, her high heels clicking on the bare boards. The door slammed behind her.

Relief flooded through Kate, followed by a certain amount of smugness. Hilary had been outplayed and Guides would take place tonight. The situation had been rescued. She turned toward Baden, her thanks rising to her lips.

His clear blue gaze hooked hers. Suddenly she was acutely conscious of his height, his sharply appraising gaze and the unasked questions on his face. Questions that demanded answers.

Her stomach dropped to the floor. Her private life had just collided with her working life.

She'd wanted to keep the two completely separate. No way was she going to tell him about her battle with the town and relive the horror of the last year. But Warragurra's size was conspiring to throw them together.

The exhilaration of the rescue faded fast, leaving dread in its wake.

* * *

Baden had supervised the beating of batter, tossed a hundred pancakes, wiped up more sugar than an army of ants could have consumed and had fought off sixteen girls attacking him with teatowel flicks.

But now peace reigned. Their parents had collected all the Guides and Sasha had gone with Erin for an ice-cream treat on the way home. Although why Erin's mother thought they needed any more food after the feast they'd just had was beyond him. But apparently ice cream was a must with pancakes, even if the ice cream had to be consumed half an hour after the pancakes.

As he folded up the last trestle table he surreptitiously watched Kate, or Koala, as the Guides called her. She wore a vivid pink and blue apron over her casual uniform and flour stuck to her forehead.

Her silky smooth hair, which normally hung in a perfect curve around her face at work, had been pulled back in a blue hair tie. Tendrils had escaped and now stuck to her cheeks, which were bright pink from the heat in the hall. She looked about eighteen. Except for the fine lines around her eyes.

Lines that life had put there. He recognised them, he had some of his own and many more than he'd had two years ago.

Did they have anything to do with the standoff he'd witnessed when he'd arrived earlier in the evening? The moment he and Sasha had walked into the hall he'd recognised the vitriol on Hilary Smithton's face.

And every protective instinct he possessed had gone into overdrive. The intensity of his response had left him stunned. The only other time he'd experienced such feelings had been when Sasha had been a toddler and a large dog had bared its teeth at her.

But Kate wasn't a toddler so this reaction was foolish. Most of him wanted to run a mile. Kate belonged at work. He had no plans to get involved with anyone again. Love was unreliable and he had to protect Sasha.

He'd kept all their conversations at work firmly centred on work. Hell, he hadn't even realised she was the Guide leader until Sasha had mentioned it two minutes before they'd arrived. Spending an evening with Kate hadn't been part of his plan for tonight, but the twist of Hilary's mouth, and the venom of her words, had made him speak.

Kate had treated the episode with Hilary as if it hadn't happened and now, two hours later, he was none the wiser as to the reason for Hilary's antipathy. The Guide meeting had continued as smoothly as if there had never been a threat to the evening.

'Cup of tea?' Kate held out a steaming mug.

'In this heat?' He bit off the words. 'Are you insane?'

She smiled, 'Ah, but it makes you feel cooler.'

'What, after it's made you twice as hot?' He eyed the hot drink with distrust.

'That's right.' She laughed, a mellow, throaty sound. 'Are you judging my mother's logic?'

He stamped down on the rush of pleasure that streaked through him at the sound of her laugh. 'Yes, I am.'

She sank down into a chair, all grace and innate elegance, which was at odds with her current bedraggled look. 'You're right, it's crazy thinking but there's nothing cool in the fridge and I need a cup of tea.'

The thought of a cold beer materialised in his head. 'After sixteen giggling girls and a run-in with Hilary Smithton, you probably need something stronger than that.'

She flinched as if she'd been struck and her relaxed demeanour vanished. 'No, I just need to sit down and catch my breath.' The words came out precise and clipped as she put her mug down by her chair.

It was obvious she didn't want to talk about it. And, hell, he didn't really want to know because asking meant involving himself in her life. He didn't want to be involved in her life. Getting involved with a woman wasn't part of the plan, couldn't be part of the plan. He and Sasha were doing fine on their own.

But something more than curiosity pushed him to ask. 'Why does Hilary Smithton hate you?'

He heard her sharp intake of breath and the scrape of her chair aginst the floorboards. 'I really appreciate you helping me out tonight, Baden. You saved the girls from disappointment and helped three of them get their cooking badge.' Her mouth curved upwards in a smile so tight it threatened to break in half.

Irritation chafed him. 'You're avoiding my question.'

'I'm not sure it's one you have the right to ask.' Coolness clung to the words like frost.

Indignation spluttered inside him, quickly taking hold. He'd bailed her out. That alone deserved an explanation. Now she was treating him as if he was the person who'd treated her so rudely. Righteous anger spurred him on to speak. 'If this issue with Hilary is going to affect Sasha's safety then I have the right to ask and the right to demand an answer.'

Her shoulders stiffened. 'I would *never* jeopardise the safety of the girls. Ever.'

Frustration collided with guilt. Intrinsically he knew she spoke the truth. She was right. Sasha would be safe at Guides. Irritation prickled at the realisation that he'd been out of line. In this situation he didn't have the right to ask that question.

At work it would be totally different. He'd have the right to demand an explanation, especially if it affected her performance. And should it ever happen, he would invoke that right. But this wasn't work.

This time he had to let it go.

The fact that bothered him so much upset him even more.

Kate counted silently backwards from ten as Warragurra airstrip seemed to rise up to meet them. Glen brought the plane down smoothly onto the runway, a tiny bump the only sensation that they weren't still in the air. She loved it when she got to zero in her counting just as the plane landed.

'Kate, can you write up your proposal for a "Pit Stop" Field Day at Coonbunga Station?' Baden unbuckled his harness.

'You think it's worth pursuing?'

'Absolutely.' Enthusiasm moved across his face. 'It combines health education, screening and personalised health information. Plus you've tapped into people's competitiveness and made it fun. I think they'll enjoy themselves and learn a lot as they put their bodies through a safety check and determine their "airworthiness". It's a brilliant idea.'

A thrill tripped though her at his praise. A thrill totally connected to his professional recognition of her idea. It was great to be part of a team with a supportive colleague. 'Thanks. I'm glad you liked it.'

'It's really innovative, Kate. Well done.' He stood up, his smile washing over her, his height seeming to fill the plane.

The lingering warmth from his praise immediately flared, spiralling into waves of heat.

Exactly how long are you going to kid yourself that feelings like this are from professional recognition?

She hummed to herself, drowning out the voice of reason. They worked together. Nothing could happen. She wouldn't allow anything to happen. Not that she had to worry. If she was honest with herself, it was only a one-way attraction. All her way. She could kid herself that his bone-melting smiles were especially directed at her but she'd seen him smile at everyone in much the same way. Except for Sasha.

When he was with Sasha his aura of a wide personal space seemed to vanish. Lightness came into his eyes chasing away the gloom that sometimes hovered around him. It seemed crazy but she had this feeling that when he smiled at Sasha she was seeing the image of the man he had once been.

Since the night at the Guide Hall ten days ago, when she'd frostily refused to tell him about Hilary, he'd been slightly more aloof than before. That niggled at her. And it drove her mad that it did. She'd respected his silence and hadn't asked him about Sasha's mother. So why did he feel he could be grumpy with her when she kept her private life private, just like he did?

Yet at three o'clock in the morning she was often lying awake, listening to the hum of the air-conditioner and thinking about why Baden and Sasha were on their own.

Thinking about Baden.

About how it would feel to tangle her fingers in his thick black curls. How it would feel to explore golden skin stretched taut over toned muscle.

Suddenly her skin prickled with heat. She quickly exited the plane into a hot, dry wind. At least the forty-degree Celsius day was good for something! It hid the source of her being hot and bothered.

Baden's long stride quickly caught her up but the wind prevented any conversation. As he opened the door into the offices for her, she breathed in deeply, deliberately catching his fresh and spicy scent.

Regret poured through her the moment she did it. 'I'll start on the proposal tonight. See you tomorrow.' She turned toward her office, thankful to be able to put some physical space between herself and Baden and find some equilibrium for her jangled emotions.

He checked his watch. 'Can I ask a favour? I got a ride here this morning from Jenkin's Mechanics. Can you give me a ride back into town?'

Dismay filled her at the unexpected request. She wanted to say no. Baden in her small car was so much closer than Baden in the plane. But no wasn't an option. She tried to sound casual. 'Sure, no problem.'

'Great, thanks. I'll just grab some stuff from the office.' He strode down the hall, the cotton twill of his trousers outlining the tightness of his buttocks.

Kate closed her eyes, refusing to stare, but the after-image burned brightly in her mind.

Five minutes later Baden folded his body into her sports car, appreciation and intrigue written clearly on his face. 'I've always wanted a car like this.' He ran his finger along the dashboard.

She grimaced. 'It's up for sale if you're interested.'

'Really?' For a moment consideration crossed his face but it faded as quickly as it had come. 'Sasha's tennis team would have to ride on the roof. Pity, though. It must be fun to drive. Why are you selling it?'

Because getting rid of this car is part of my new life. 'It's not practical.' She quickly reversed out of the parking space and pulled onto the road.

'But no one buys a car like this out of practicality. Why did you buy it?' He swivelled slightly in his seat, his attention completely focussed on her.

'I didn't buy it.' Shane's blotchy face hovered in her mind. *Katie, baby, don't leave me.* Her fingers tightened on the steering-wheel. 'It was a…' *Bribe.* 'It was a gift.'

He whistled. 'Lucky you.'

'That's your opinion.' The muttered words left her mouth before her brain had the sense to cut them off.

His black brows immediately rose, interest clearly etched on his handsome face.

The Jenkin's Mechanics sign thankfully came into view and she pulled up onto the concrete apron. 'Here we are.'

Baden opened the door. 'Thanks for the ride.'

'You're welcome.' She flicked the switch to open the boot so he could get his bag.

He climbed out of the car and paused, bending down to talk to her. 'By the way, Jen asked me to remind you that the dinner for the new physiotherapist is going to be at the Royal.' He inclined his head in the direction of the building across the road.

The newly furbished Royal Hotel was a popular place catering for the coffee and cake set through to discerning diners in the grand dining room. The sports bar with its many large plasma screens had been cleverly contained within a heritage façade. From the outside people glimpsed the Warragurra of old when silver had lined its streets and money had been no object. The renovation had been Shane's last job with Kennedy Constructions.

Out of the corner of her eye she saw three men walk out of the back door of the hotel. Her chest tightened as she instantly recognised two of the men. The tallest of the three—Josh Martin—had been Shane's closest mate, and the best man at their wedding.

A prickle of unease ran through her. She'd avoided this part of town since coming home. Every nerve ending screamed at her to leave. She turned on the ignition.

The noise of the car made Josh look up. His lip curled when he caught sight of her.

Leave now. Do not pass go, do not collect two hundred dollars. She put the car into first gear.

Josh and the other man stepped onto the road, supporting Richie Santini, who stumbled, his gait unsteady. As they reached the middle of the road Richie slumped between them, falling against Josh and making him stagger.

A shiver of disgust ran through her. Richie was drunk again. Some things never changed. She willed them to move quickly across the road so she could get away.

'Richie!' Josh's worried voice carried across the street. 'Mate, come on, you'll get run over.'

Kate expected Richie to stand up as Josh jolted him with his body. He didn't. His colour had gone from florid to white to blue.

Hell, he was unconscious. Kate pushed her door open. 'Baden!' she called to him as his hand touched the doorhandle of the shop door. 'Quick, over here.' She ran toward the grass verge where Josh had laid Richie down.

Baden caught up to her, his medical bag in his hand.

'Roll him on his side, Josh,' Kate called out as she reached them.

Josh turned the moment he heard her voice, pure hatred lining his face. 'Get away from here, Kate. You've done enough damage.'

His words pounded her like hailstones, but he couldn't hurt her any more. No more than he and Shane had already. And another person didn't deserve to die.

'Don't be stupid, Josh. I'm a nurse. I can help.' She dropped to her knees to check Richie's airway, the stench of stale alcohol almost making her retch.

Josh's arm shot out from his side, striking her across the shoulder in an attempt to push her away.

She gasped, desperately trying to maintain her balance as pain and the past swamped her.

'Step back from her. Now!' Baden's voice boomed out like a sergeant major establishing control. 'I'm a doctor and I'm in charge.' He pointed to the unknown man. 'You. Restrain your mate before I flatten him.'

Through the fog of shock Kate realised the experienced triage doctor had just secured the scene.

'Kate.'

He spoke her name with caring firmness, centring her. She swung around to face him as if he were a lifeline in a storm-ravaged sea.

His expression was neutral but his eyes swirled with eddies of fury tinged with disbelief. 'Kate, call an ambulance.' He tossed her his phone and immediately turned his attention to the patient, implementing what Kate had tried to do—assess the airway, check the breathing and the circulation.

She stood up and walked five steps away. With trembling fingers she managed to dial 000.

Josh took a step forward.

Kate stood her ground but her grip on the mobile phone threatened to crush it.

His mate put his hand on Josh's shoulder. 'Give them space to do their job, Josh.'

'I am, Trev.' Josh tried to shrug off his hand.

The dispatcher finally answered. 'Police, fire or ambulance?'

'Ambulance.' She wanted the police but that would only make things worse.

Baden called out to her. 'No pulse. Commencing CPR now.'

She nodded, indicating she'd heard him. The professional nurse kicked back in, corralling her shock and fear into a place to be dealt with later. 'We have a collapsed patient with no pulse. Doctor in attendance and CPR commenced. We need a defibrillator.'

'Hell, Richie.' Josh's voice cracked as Baden's arms pushed against Richie's chest, compressing his heart, attempting to get it pumping again.

Kate ended the call and knelt down next to Baden.

His firm voice counted the compressions. 'Twenty-six, twenty-seven, twenty-eight, twenty-nine, thirty.'

She blew two breaths through the Laerdal pocket mask into Richie's mouth and checked for a pulse. 'No pulse. Keep compressing.' She strained her ears for the ambulance. 'We need that defibrillator now.'

They established a rhythm, with Baden compressing and Kate giving the rescue breaths, but she knew how physical CPR was and how arms tired quickly. 'Swap at thirty?'

Baden nodded, still counting, keeping the beat of thirty compressions to two breaths.

The swap had to be fluid. The recent guideline changes for CPR focussed on more compressions with fewer interruptions.

Kate started counting out loud. 'Twenty-eight, twenty-nine, thirty. Change.' Her crossed hands immediately started compressions where Baden's had been. *Don't die on me, Richie.*

But she knew the reality. She'd seen his swollen ankles—unusual in a man in his mid-thirties. His heart muscle was saggy and overstretched, its capacity to start again severely compromised by a lifetime of binge drinking.

A small crowd had gathered, including Baden's mechanic, Scott. All of them stood watching with a mixture of fascination and horror as a life hung in the balance.

'Change of heart, Katie?' Josh's cruel voice exploded above her. 'Saving Rich won't make up for the fact you killed Shane.'

His words struck her as hard as a physical blow. Blood pooled in her feet, silver lights exploded in her head and she started to shake. *Concentrate on the job.*

She counted loudly, the words and the rhythm driving away her fear, allowing her wavering courage a chance to take hold.

'Scott, get him out of here or I'm calling the police.'

Raging fury poured through Baden's words. 'This isn't daytime TV drama.'

Kate heard the barely audible aside as he lowered his head to give Richie another rescue breath.

Except it was her past life unfolding in all its sordid detail in front of the one man she'd wanted to keep it from.

Five men surrounded Josh and guided him to one side as the ambulance screamed to a halt. The paramedic and an intern from the base hospital ran to them, carrying the portable defibrillator.

A flurry of hands worked on Richie. Kate kept compressing while the paramedics attached the monitor pads.

'He's in asystole.' Michael, the doctor, interpreted the readout.

'Shock him now,' Baden instructed as he reached for the intravenous kit.

'Stand clear.' Michael discharged electrical current into Richie's chest.

The monitor flatlined.

'Resume compressions.' Baden nodded to Kate. 'Prepare for stacked shocks.' He slid the butterfly cannula into Richie's arm and drew up adrenaline. 'I don't have a good feeling about this.'

He wasn't telling her anything she didn't already know. The odds were stacked against getting an exhausted heart muscle to start beating again.

'Stand clear.' Michael pressed the button and the pads delivered another shock to Richie's chest.

All eyes focussed on the readout.

'We've got a wobbly rhythm.' Michael sounded uncertain.

'Thank God.' Kate's softly spoken words came out on a breath. He had a second chance.

'Yeah, but for how long?' Baden's bald words indicated the reality of the situation.

'Let's transfer him immediately. He needs every bit of expertise Coronary Care can provide.' Michael nodded to the paramedic. 'On my count.'

They lifted the heavy man onto the stretcher and transferred him into the rig. Michael clambered in to monitor Richie and his co-worker switched on the siren and drove them away.

Kate's legs immediately started to shake, followed by her arms and then the rest of her body. Bile scalded her throat as she gulped in air, trying to still her heaving stomach.

She saw Josh being hustled away but not before he looked straight at her and used his arm to make an offensive gesture.

Baden's strong arm curled around her, pulling her in close. 'It's over now, Kate.' He spoke softly, his words comforting as his hand stroked her hair.

She needed to go, needed to leave this minute. She shouldn't be standing here. She shouldn't want to be in Baden's arms, seeking shelter. She shouldn't want to lay her head on his chest and close her eyes and forget. Forget everything except the touch of his body against hers, the rise and fall of his chest against her breasts and his heat flooding into rekindling sensations she'd long forgotten.

For one brief moment she gave in to temptation, resting her head on his shoulder, feeling the softness of his cotton shirt against her cheek and the hardness of the muscle underneath. Taking a sample to last her for ever.

She wrenched herself away. She had to go before he asked questions. Asked difficult questions she didn't want to answer. 'I have to go.'

His hand gripped her arm. 'You're not going anywhere without me.'

The firmness of his voice startled her. She looked up into navy eyes filled with a hard edge she didn't recognise. Apprehension rippled through her. 'I'm fine, really. I'll make myself a cup of tea with loads of sugar.' She forced a smile onto her face, hoping to placate him.

The flash in his eyes said he'd seen straight through her ploy. 'It's not just you I'm worried about. When your private life impinges on a patient's well-being then it's no longer private. We're going somewhere quiet and you're going to tell me what the hell is going on with you and this town.'

Panic clawed at her as Shane's legacy reared again, determined to haunt her. She desperately tried to think of a way of avoiding this meeting. She opened her mouth to speak and closed it again.

Determination lined Baden's face. He wouldn't let her go until she agreed to his demand.

At that precise moment she knew she had no choice.

CHAPTER FOUR

BADEN sat on a wicker seat, sipping lemon, lime and bitters, under a thick green canopy of twining wisteria. He had the surreal feeling he'd stepped back in time.

He could feel a stream of cool air at his back, coming from inside the homestead's thick russet and ochre stone walls. In front of him an unexpectedly green lawn sloped down toward the river and the magnificent red river gums. Hundreds of years old, one of their gnarled trunks looked as if it had regrown around the site where Aborigines had once carved a canoe.

Weeping peppercorn trees and towering jacarandas softened the harsh stone lines of the house and perfume from the extensive rose garden scented the early evening air. Visions wafted through his head—people chatting on the lawn, ladies promenading in white muslin dresses, men in suits, a jazz band playing and flappers doing the Charleston on the dock by the river. Their laughing voices echoed around him, memories of the jubilant celebrations of a successful wool clip in days long gone when the merino sheep had been gold on four legs.

He couldn't believe Kate lived in the Sandon homestead, one of Warragurra's eminent homes. A home with a round National Trust plaque at the front door and neatly beneath it a Kennedy Constructions historic brass renovation plate.

How had he not known she lived here? *You never asked.* He hadn't wanted to ask, scared if he did so he'd become even more intrigued by her. Even so, he wasn't certain Kate would have divulged the information freely.

She'd insisted that the only place she would talk to him was at her home. And what a home it was. He remembered Annie showing him an article and photographs from a lifestyle magazine about the house and the million-dollar renovation. It had been around the time they'd first discussed moving to Warragurra. He'd joked at the time that he'd buy it for her if it ever came on the market.

But Annie had never made it to Warragurra or to Sandon homestead. Her illness-ravaged body had succumbed before the final plans had been in place. A twinge of guilt tugged at him that he was here now and that the woman in front of him intrigued him and filled his dreams.

Kate sat opposite him, wound as tight as a drum, with waves of tension rolling off her.

His anger and disgust at the events of the afternoon had abated but the sensation of holding Kate in his arms, her breasts pressed firmly against his chest, the silky feeling of her hair under his fingers, had stayed strong.

Too strong. Too vivid.

When he'd pulled her into his arms he hadn't thought, he'd just acted. She'd looked like she had been about to faint on the pavement. Holding her had been the most natural thing in the world. But want had quickly drowned empathy as her heat had flowed into him.

He hadn't held a woman for two years. He hadn't wanted to hold a woman in that time. Not until today. The guilt dug in deeper as his hazy memory tried valiantly to recall Annie's feel and touch. It came up blank against the vivid feel of Kate.

He ran his hand across the back of his neck. Now wasn't the time to be changing his game plan—his top priority had to be Sasha. That meant keeping his distance from Kate. This was work and the only reason he was here was to find out what the hell was going on in this town.

But asking her outright would just make her defensive so he approached it gently. 'I bet this place saw some parties. I almost feel we should be sipping gin and tonics in deference to the house.'

She raised her brows. 'This house has a long history of wild parties, right up until a year ago.'

He put his glass down on the red gum table. 'Really? What changed?'

She sighed a long shuddering breath. 'Shane...my husband died.'

A dull ache flared then throbbed inside him. He knew the excruciating pain of loss too well. 'I'm so sorry.'

Stunned disbelief scored her face at his well-meant sentiment.

Remorse immediately tugged at him. He'd just exacerbated her pain. 'Words don't do a damn thing to help, do they?'

She blinked, her large eyes swirling with undecipherable emotions. 'Actually, sorry isn't a word I've heard very much, so thank you.'

Bewilderment lurched through him. 'Your husband died and people didn't say sorry?'

She shifted in her seat, folding and unfolding her arms before standing up. 'Seeing as you're insisting we have this conversation, can we do it while we walk in the garden?'

Conflicting needs clashed. His need to know what was going on collided with Kate's evident pain at having to tell him, and meanwhile the clock ticked on. He had to collect Sasha from the pool at seven. He sighed. 'Look, you don't need to tell me your life story and I don't want to cause you a lot of grief by asking you to revisit your tragic loss.

'But whatever's going on between you and the people in this town, it's now impacting on your job. So that involves me. The only thing I need to know is why the people in the town dislike you so much.'

She gave a brittle laugh. 'The *only* thing? I wish it was that simple.' She swallowed hard. 'They blame me for Shane's death.'

Thoughts tumbled through his mind. Car accident? Medical emergency? 'Why?'

Kate started striding quickly toward the river, shredding a eucalyptus leaf with her fingers as she walked, the strong, fresh aroma of the oil trailing behind her. She caught his gaze, her expression a mixture of culpability and distress. 'Oh, God, there's no easy way to tell you this.'

Her vulnerability rocked him. The desire to pull her into his arms, stroke her hair and ease her pain surged through him, immediate and strong. He clenched his hands to keep his arms by his sides. He didn't want to cause her any more pain and part of him wanted to say, Don't tell me, I don't need to know.

But he did. As her boss, he had to know.

Just listen. Support her by listening. 'Start at the beginning if it helps.'

She threw him a grateful look. 'You asked me on my first day back at work if I was Kate Kennedy. Well, I was for five years. I married Shane, the eldest son of the Kennedy family.'

The image of her flashing eyes the day he'd questioned her surname rushed through his mind. 'Would I be right if I guessed the construction Kennedys?' Suddenly where she lived started to make sense.

She nodded. 'That's right. Warragurra establishment. Kennedys have been building Warragurra buildings for a very long time. Shane used to take pleasure in the fact he was often renovating buildings his great-grandfather had built.

'He was a gifted craftsman and his talent was bringing buildings back to life so they shone. At the same time he gave people the opportunity to value the past, while giving them the modern conveniences. He and I renovated Sandon.'

'Did a love of heritage buildings bring you together?' He asked the question, the drive to know more about her straining at his self-imposed restraint.

Her lips tugged slightly at the corners. 'That and his wicked sense of humour. Shane was a funny guy. He was the bloke you'd ask to be MC at a fundraising dinner or a wedding. He was larger than life, he had an air of excitement about him and he didn't take things too seriously. I was working at the base hospital in those days and I think after a day in ICU where life and death can sit so closely together I found him to be a breath of fresh air.'

Her breath shuddered out of her lungs. 'I completely missed the dark side of him, the opposite side of the larger-than-life, fun-loving guy.'

Baden probed gently. 'Was he depressed?'

She hesitated for a few seconds. 'My husband was a hidden alcoholic.'

He tried to keep his face neutral as the unanticipated words settled around them.

Her voice wavered. 'With the exception of my colleagues, no one in this town accepts that because Shane didn't fit the stereotype. He held down a great job, he was well respected in the community and he managed a complex business with his father. But every night he would drink.'

He spoke quietly. 'That can't have been easy.'

A flutter of hurt surfaced briefly in her eyes until she blinked.

She stared ahead. 'At first it was a few beers, and then it was beer and a bottle of wine. Business lunches got added into the mix until he could consume up to four bottles of wine a day plus beer and spirits. His personality at home became dramatically different from his public persona. The man I married had completely disappeared, submerged in a sea of alcohol.'

Her despair radiated through Baden. 'That would have been really tough. What did you do?'

She threw her hands up. 'What didn't I do? I'd married for better or worse, in sickness and in health. But addiction isn't like other illnesses and there's no quick fix. It slowly pervaded every aspect of our lives and insidiously took us down into bleakness.'

He concentrated on her words, every part of him shuddering as he felt her pain.

'I asked him to cut back, I refused to have alcohol in the house, I asked him to see a doctor, have hypnotherapy, go to Alcoholics Anonymous—I even suggested couples counselling, but I was a lone voice.' She tossed her head as if shaking the past away. 'This is a country town and drinking is embedded in the fabric of the community. His mates all enjoyed a drink at the pub. No one could see anything wrong with how Shane led his life.'

Baden had worked with alcoholics before and he knew what a tough fight she must have faced. 'And he didn't see he had a problem?'

She nodded slowly. 'That's right. He didn't believe he had a drinking problem. He told me I was a killjoy and the problem was all mine. His parents refused to accept he was an alcoholic and made continual excuses for him, but mostly they just blamed me.' She puffed out a breath. 'I was difficult, I didn't understand him, I was spoilt. He worked hard, giving me a good lifestyle, so surely he deserved to relax a bit after work.' Her voice caught. 'His mates thought I was an interfering witch.'

She hugged her arms close to her and shivered, even though the late-afternoon sun seared everything in its path. 'The night he got violent and trashed the kitchen was the night I left.'

Irrational resentment toward a sick man consumed him. A man who obviously hadn't valued the wonderful woman he'd married. 'You did the right thing, Kate. No one has the right to abuse.'

She showed no sign she'd heard him, her eyes glazed with hurtful memories. She continued talking—her need to get the story told so great. 'Shane couldn't believe I'd left him. He showered me with presents, including the car; he begged me to come back and he promised me he'd change. I needed to believe he would try and I gave him a second chance.' Her haunted gaze hooked with his, pleading for him to understand.

'You loved him.' He spoke the words, trying to support her, but they unexpectedly speared him like a jagged knife.

Her fingers curled deeply into the muscles of her upper arms and when she spoke the words came out flat. 'His promise lasted a month.'

The low-life! Anger spurted through Baden like water from a geyser. Immediately the doctor in him struggled to override the strong reaction. 'He was sick, Kate.'

She nodded, swallowing hard. 'The hardest thing was knowing that until he acknowledged to himself he had a problem, nothing would change. I officially moved out. His parents harangued me, our friends stopped talking to me and his closest friends hated me.' She raised her troubled eyes to his. 'You met them today.'

The urge to touch her intensified. He wanted to show her he understood. He shoved his hands in his pockets to stop himself. 'That was a very courageous thing to do.'

'Courageous?' Her eyes widened and bitterness lined her face. 'I left him and five months later he hanged himself.'

Suicide.

Air rushed out of his lungs. He hadn't expected that at all. He'd imagined Shane had run his car off the road drunk or had experienced cardiac problems or liver complications like his friend this afternoon. He ran his hand through his hair. 'Hell, Kate, I'm sorry. Suicide leaves so many raw emotions. But surely you know Shane's death is not your fault?'

She stopped walking and stared out toward the river. 'On my good days I know that. I stayed in town for four months after Shane died but when his parents started calling me a gold-digger and tried to contest his will, life in Warragurra became almost impossible for me.'

Understanding flowed through him. 'So you went to Europe hoping things would settle, and the town thought you'd gone for good.'

She swung back to face him and gave a wry smile. 'That's right. I left needing some time and space. I know in my heart that I didn't kill Shane, but his family's hate campaign eroded my confidence, escalated my guilt.' She nibbled her bottom lip. 'But this is *my* town, too, with my friends, and it was time to come home.'

She swallowed hard, her voice trembling. 'But today was the first time Shane's closest friends have seen me, although Hilary would have told them I'd returned.'

He grappled to comprehend the tangled situation of grief, money and power. The reaction of Shane's parents seemed to be pathological grief. 'Surely his parents wouldn't have any claim to Shane's will?'

She shrugged her shoulders. 'Legally they don't but that didn't stop them from seeking advice from numerous solicitors across the country and starting a campaign against me in letters to the editor in the *Warragurra Times*. They'd lost their son, they needed to blame someone. I was the obvious person. His mother had never been thrilled about our relationship and now I was alive and her son was dead.'

'Grief drives people to do irrational things.' The words sounded bald and useless as resentment bubbled through him at the grief-driven spite of Kate's in-laws. Part of him wished he'd known her then and had been able to do something. Support her in some way.

Again she tossed her head, her silky hair swinging around her face. 'But that's all over now. I refuse to be a scapegoat. I love Warragurra. Since my parents died I've called Warragurra home. My job and my friends are here and I refuse to let a minority group drive me out. This is my new start. I will never let anyone take me down to that dark black pit of despair again.'

Her emotional bravery awed him but at the same time sadness enveloped him on her behalf. A beautiful, generous woman deserved more. A lot more. 'Not every marriage is black. It can be a wonderful thing.'

'Yes, well, I don't plan to find out.' Her eyes flashed with determination. 'I do my job well, Baden. The service supports me and as I work out of town, what you experienced today has never happened before. I doubt it will ever happen again. I'm sorry I didn't tell you when you started but I didn't think it would impact on you. I'm sorry you had to encounter my sordid past.'

Her amazing strength radiated through her words. She'd been to hell and back and yet she was apologising to him. 'I've never doubted your professionalism, Kate. As a newcomer I'm not privy to the nuances of the town. I didn't realise life here was so tough for you. I'm surprised you came back.'

She laced her fingers in front of her, pressing down so hard against the backs of her hands that her knuckles gleamed white. 'I have a right to live in this town. I love my job and my friends. I have a right to a happy, single life.' She swung one arm out wide. 'Sandon is too big for me but I won't be moved on by bigotry. When I sell, it will be my decision.'

She stood before him, firm, willowy and tall like the tree behind her. A beautiful woman facing down demons no one should ever have to deal with.

The slightest tremble vibrated along her plump bottom lip as her shoulders quivered. 'But sometimes it's so damn hard.'

He knew exactly what she meant. Sometimes it *was* too damn hard. Instantly, his resolve to keep his distance fell away. She needed his support. He needed to show her he understood. Stepping in close, he reached for her, winding his arms around her waist and drawing her close.

She stiffened in his arms.

He rested his chin against her hair. 'It's OK. We all have bad days.'

Slowly, her breath shuddered out of her lungs as she relaxed against him, languid and warm. She nestled her head into his shoulder and strands of her hair caressed his cheek. Her sweet scent encircled him as her breath fanned out against his neck.

He stroked her hair just like he stroked Sasha's when she was upset, but unlike with Sasha, an overwhelming sense of tranquillity wove through him as he held her. A sensation he'd forgotten.

As he moved his head to drop a light 'it's all better now' kiss onto her forehead, she tilted her head back. His lips collided with hers. Warm, soft lips that tasted like nectar.

Instantly the kiss changed.

His arm tightened around her waist, closing the infinitesimal space between them. Her body moulded itself to his, pressing hard against his length. All space between them vanished. So did every thought of support.

He wanted to touch her, taste her, plunder her glorious mouth, needing it as badly as a man in the desert needed water.

He slanted his mouth firmly against hers as every emotion he'd submerged since meeting her rose to the surface, demanding to be sated.

A low moan of want sounded in her throat as her lips yielded under his.

White lights exploded in his head.

Heat merged with heat.

Longing collided with need.

He lost himself in her hot, velvet mouth, which welcomed him, drawing him in, giving yet taking at the same time. His blood pounded through him, his need strong and hard, crashing easily through every barricade he'd erected.

She reached up, her breasts moving in a caressing motion, her nipples hardening against his chest. She snaked her arms around his neck, pulling his head closer still. Her fingers tangled in his hair as her mouth covered his, her tongue savouring, exploring and branding all at the same time.

The here and now fell away. Nothing existed except the two of them and their driving need.

He tore his mouth from hers and trailed kisses along her neck, tasting the salty hollow at the base of her throat and stroking the curve of her jaw.

She suddenly stepped backwards, pulling him with her as she rested against the tree. Her desire-fuelled gaze zeroed in on his face, all shadows of the past pushed aside.

Through his fog of need he knew instinctively that she wanted him as much as he wanted her.

He lifted her against the tree as her legs entwined with his, her body rising up.

Her fingers fumbled frantically with the buttons on his shirt, pulling the fabric briskly aside before resting her palms flat on his chest. A sigh of pleasure echoed around him.

His breath came in ragged jerks as sensations drove through him, exploding in bursts of pure, undiluted lust. He'd taken and conquered her mouth but he wanted more. He wanted to know how her slick and silky skin felt against his, wanted to feel the full and heavy weight of her swelling breast in his hand, he wanted her legs high around his waist and to truly feel her. He wanted to take her right now under the magnificent stately red river gum with its heady scent of eucalyptus.

This is crazy.

But he was past listening.

He pushed her shirt from her shoulders. Smooth, flawless skin greeted him, her breasts round and full, her nipples hard with longing. Groaning, he lowered his head, fixing his mouth around the enticing softness, his tongue flicking her nipple.

Her hands gripped his head hard as she bucked against him. A delicious moan of longing left her lips.

She wants this as much as you do.

He lifted her up, supporting them against the tree, cupping her with his hand, burying his face in her neck.

Nothing mattered except their need. Their need to push the past away and lose themselves in each other.

The shrill sound of a phone ringing split the air.

His phone.

The here and now slammed into him so fast it winded him. Kate pulled back, her chest heaving. 'You'd better take that.'

He nodded mutely and lowered her to her feet before

pressing the answer button on his mobile phone. 'Hello?' His husky voice could hardly speak.

'Dad, where are you? It's way past seven.' Sasha's indignant voice sounded down the line.

Sasha. All his blood drained from his head and he swayed. He'd completely forgotten Sasha.

Guilt slammed into him with a sickening thud. He ran his hand over the back of his neck. What the hell was wrong with him? How could he have forgotten his daughter?

Promise me you'll always make Sasha your top priority. Annie's words seared him.

He'd just allowed lust to completely take over. He'd been behaving like a teenager. He was a grown man, a doctor, a father, and yet he'd been seducing his nurse in her garden. *Oh, yeah, that's really classy.*

His guilt solidified. 'I'll be there in ten minutes, sweetheart.' He punched the 'off' button.

He turned back to Kate. She stood a short distance from the tree, her blouse rebuttoned and tucked in, her natural elegance and grace giving her a serene calmness. But her swollen lips clearly told the real story, reminding him of their recent folly.

He forced himself to speak. 'I'm sorry.'

'Yes.' A muscle twitched in her jaw.

God, he felt like a louse. He'd taken advantage of a woman in an emotionally vulnerable state, but at the same time every cell in his body screamed for him to leave. 'I'm sorry, I have to go.'

'Of course you do.' Her smile didn't quite reach her eyes where the shadows marched in formation, reclaiming their rightful place.

CHAPTER FIVE

'MORNING, Baden.' Kate forced the words out praying they sounded casual as well as bright and breezy.

'Morning, Kate. How are you?'

'Good. Yourself?'

'Fine. How's Sasha?'

'She's well, thank you.' Baden's deep voice vibrated with a new reserve.

Tension circled Kate like a boa constrictor. The clipped conversation dripped with unspoken words. Words neither of them wanted to speak.

Many people dreaded Monday morning but she wasn't usually one of them. She loved a new week, all fresh and shiny, ready to be embraced. But not today. On Friday she'd more than embraced Baden. She'd been a hair's breadth away from total abandonment.

Her cheeks flamed at the thought. She'd spent the weekend dreading this morning, knowing she would have to face him. Work with him all day, all week and well into the year.

She'd spent the weekend unable to settle to anything, constantly replaying the moment a simple and kindly sympathetic embrace had fired into the most sensual kiss she'd ever known.

How could one mouth create so many emotions and destroy every particle of her willpower? With one kiss she'd melted against him, every cell in her body humming with an all-consuming yearning to touch him and feel him in every way possible.

She'd completely yielded to the wondrous sensations his mouth had ignited deep inside her, letting them take over absolutely, leading her as a willing follower. She'd lost track of time and place and propriety. She would have made love to him under the river red gum without a moment's hesitation.

The thought both appealed and appalled. She was a grown woman, not a sixteen-year-old with more sex drive than sense. And yet her body had craved him with such force she'd hardly recognised herself.

But had she misread the situation? Had she been the one driving the kiss? The horrified expression that had streaked across his handsome face when his phone had rung had whipped her so hard she could still feel the sting.

He'd realised with stunning clarity what he had been doing and who he had been doing it with. Guilt had scored his face and he'd run so fast from her there was a possibility he'd broken records. Was it to do with Sasha's mother? Or was it all to do with her? Getting involved with Kate Kennedy would make his life in the town difficult. She bit her lip. Most of her understood. A small part railed against it.

So exactly what did you say to your boss post–thwarted seduction?

'Do you have the test results for Lucinda Masterton?' Baden slid into his seat, fastening his safety harness, his face impassive.

You talk about work and nothing else.

As the plane taxied down the runway she opened her briefcase. 'I do and I'll be signing her up for my next diabetes education group.'

Baden nodded. 'Good idea. Have you followed up Caroline Lovett? Emily was concerned about her.'

'I telephoned her last week but if she isn't at this morning's clinic I will personally go and collect her.'

'What, in Cameron's ute?' Azure eyes twinkled with a wicked glint.

It was the first sign he'd shown that morning of the Baden she'd grown used to. 'Betsy is the perfect example that you don't need doors for the engine to work.'

He laughed, the tension on his body sliding away. His face relaxed, his high cheekbones softened, even his curls seemed to unwind, brushing against his forehead.

Liquid heat flowed through her right down to her toes. She adjusted her position in the seat, disconcerted by her strong response. In the confined space of the plane her legs collided with his, her foot tangling behind his left calf.

Immediately Baden's rigid tension returned, coiling through him like a snake ready to strike. His eyes darkened to a stormy blue.

Piercing regret stabbed her. She'd just glimpsed the future. Working with Baden had changed for ever. She cleared her throat and focussed. Opening the next folder, she continued, 'I want to refer Prani Veejit to the endocrine unit at the base hospital because of her thyroxine levels.'

Monday morning's mid-air case conference had begun, the first task in a busy day.

Four hours later, Kate stretched her back after working non-stop in cramped conditions. The places she set up her clinics never ceased to amaze her. Today she was in the footy clubroom's kitchen with her portable steriliser and her folding examination table. It was the only room that offered a door that closed and privacy. Space in the kitchen was at a premium and she swore her spine had connected with the black handles of the ancient pie warmer every time she'd carried out the pap test examinations.

Her well-women's clinic had been full as it had been a long time since the service had been offered in the remote community of Gemton. She'd just seen the last patient on her long list. The health clinic doubled as a social event as many of these women lived on remote cattle stations and didn't see each other very often.

Each time Kate had gone out to the main hall to call in the next client she'd felt like she had been interrupting a party. Everyone had brought food—club sandwiches, mini-quiches, fruit platters—and the giant urn bubbled with boiling water for the numerous cups of tea that were required. Kate wouldn't need dinner tonight after consuming far too much delicious passionfruit sponge.

'Cup of tea, Kate?' Esther Lucas stood with a large stainless-steel teapot hovering over a mug.

'That would be lovely, thank you.'

The older woman smiled and poured the tea. 'You've had a big day today. I wonder if the doctor has seen as many men as you saw of us women.' She passed the tea and a plate of sandwiches.

Kate laughed. 'That's why Baden set up at the pub, so he has a better chance of finding the men. In general, women are better at having check-ups.'

Esther leaned forward, inclining her head. 'Not everyone saw you today who should.' She spoke conspiratorially. 'Can you take your cuppa and go have an encouraging chat to Brenda?'

'Sure, if you think I should.'

'I do, dear. Brenda's struggling. The drought has hit them hard and she's putting everyone and everything ahead of herself. She only popped in to give Tilly her birthday present but seeing as she's here…'

Country caring. It never ceased to amaze Kate how a community could care so much. She'd experienced both ends of the spectrum of small towns. This was the end that kept her going and helped maintain her faith.

As she took her tea and sandwiches toward Brenda she caught sight of Baden, who'd just arrived from his clinic. Many of the women immediately gathered around him, overwhelming him with hospitality and battering him with questions.

'Cup of tea, Doctor?'

'Did you get my Geoff to talk to you?'

'Have some sponge or perhaps a sandwich?'

'How's that gorgeous daughter of yours? I bet she's growing up.'

Kate heard the rumble of his deep voice as he politely replied to their questions. She sighed. With them his voice was friendly and open, in stark contrast to the cool and clipped tones he'd used with her that morning.

She took in a deep breath and rolled her shoulders back. None of that mattered. What mattered was that Esther was worried about Brenda and she needed to find out why.

Brenda sat in a chair, her eyes closed and her shoulders slumped. Her workworn hands lay folded in her lap against a pair of faded jeans. A voluminous peasant-style blouse settled over her, not quite hiding a large stomach.

Kate started at Brenda's appearance. In the eight months since she'd last seen her, the woman, in her mid-forties, had gained a lot of weight. Still, that could happen as women approached menopause. She sat down next to her. 'More tired than usual, Brenda?'

Brenda opened her eyes, her mouth curving into a half-smile. 'Kate, you're back. It's good to see you.'

'Thanks, Brenda. How are things with you?'

The woman shrugged. 'You know.'

Kate spoke gently. 'No, I don't really know. How about you tell me?'

She gave a long sigh. 'We're buying in feed, the price of beef has fallen though the floor and Des is looking worse than me.' Her thumbs rolled around each other in her lap. 'I'm up at five and in bed at eleven. I'm so damn tired that I can hardly put one leg in front of the other, but that's normal, right?'

Kate hedged. 'Maybe. But it's always worth investigating so while you're here and I'm here, how about a check-up? I'll do a physical, take some blood and then we'll know if it's just the stress of the drought.'

A shimmer of fear ran through the woman's eyes. 'Des said the doc was aiming to head out by two.'

Kate rolled her eyes and grinned. 'He's so busy being fed by his fans over there that we won't be able to get away in under half an hour.' She stood up, giving Brenda an expectant look.

'I forgot how pushy you could be. All right, let's get this over, then.' Brenda slowly lumbered to her feet and walked to the kitchen.

Kate closed the door firmly behind her. She started off with non-invasive checks of pulse and blood pressure, hoping the familiarity of such routine tests would put Brenda at ease. 'Still having periods?'

Brenda nodded. 'Although they're a bit hit and miss and for the first time in my life I'm getting pain.'

Kate jotted down the word 'pain' on Brenda's history. 'Just with your period or mid-cycle?'

'Both, I guess.' Brenda looked down at her feet. 'It hurts now and then and during sex. Not that I feel like it very often, I'm so damn tired and nauseated.' She threw her head up, despair flashing in her eyes. 'I think I'm pregnant.' She lifted her shirt to expose a bloated abdomen. 'Kate, I can't be pregnant, not now, not at forty-four.'

'Let's do a pregnancy test, then.' Kate handed her a specimen jar.

Brenda grimaced. 'That won't be a problem. I'm needing to pee all the time.'

A few minutes later both women peered at the negative result.

'Well, we've ruled out one thing.' Kate smiled at Brenda. 'So now I'll do the rest of the check-up.'

'I can't wait for that.' With a resigned expression Brenda got undressed and lay down on the examination couch. 'At least in this heat your hands won't be cold.'

Kate checked Brenda's breasts for lumps, checking carefully above and below the breast as well as in the lymph nodes under the arms. 'That's all fine. Now I'm going to feel your tummy.'

She carefully pressed down on Brenda's swollen abdomen, feeling for the ovaries. A lump met her fingers. A sliver of concern whipped through her. She palpated again. The lump remained.

She needed to do a bi-manual examination but if what she suspected did exist, Baden would have to examine her. It would be better if Brenda only had to have one vaginal examination. 'Brenda, I'd really like Baden to do an internal examination.'

'Why can't you do it? You always do it.' Brenda stiffened, instantly wary.

She fudged the answer. 'I'm a bit rusty after six months off.'

Brenda's eyes narrowed as if she didn't believe her, but she nodded her head slowly. 'OK.'

Kate tucked the modesty sheet around Brenda. 'I'll just go and get him.'

Baden was still surrounded by the women of the district but

he turned toward her as soon as he heard the door open. His dark brows rose in question.

She nodded. It was uncanny how often he anticipated her or knew she wanted to discuss something with him.

'Excuse me, ladies. Thanks so much for the late lunch, it was delicious.' He walked over to her. 'How can I help?'

'I've got Brenda Cincotta presenting with erratic periods, nausea, indigestion, urinary frequency, dyspareunia and lower back pain, and on abdominal palpation I can feel a mass. It might be an ovarian cyst.' Her optimism floundered under his intense gaze.

'What did the pelvic tell you?' A fine tremor rippled through his voice.

'I haven't done it. If I felt the mass then you would have to repeat the procedure and I'm trying to avoid her having two vaginal exams. I said I was a bit rusty.'

He cleared his throat. 'I doubt she bought that.'

She shrugged. 'She didn't, but she agreed.'

'Right, well I'll examine her.' He turned and put his hand on the doorhandle then paused, perfectly still. For the briefest moment an unusual expression twisted his face and then he breathed in deeply and rolled his shoulders back.

With a jerk he opened the door and stepped through, a strained smile on his lips. 'Good to see you, Brenda. I caught up with Des today. Sorry to hear the drought is messing you about but I'm really pleased you're both taking a bit of time to look after yourselves.' He pulled on a pair of gloves. 'Kate tells me that things have been a bit haywire with your cycle just recently.'

Brenda grimaced. 'I thought I was pregnant but perhaps it's just early menopause.'

'Let's find out, shall we?'

'I need to get back, and Des has to hand-feed tonight so just get it over.' Brenda lay back and closed her eyes.

Baden gently proceeded with the examination, starting with palpation of her abdomen and then moving on to the internal.

Kate kept her gaze fixed on his face the entire time, searching for clues. His behaviour at the door had mystified her. Now an unexpected sheen of sweat broke out on his brow as his face paled.

He stripped off his gloves and handed Brenda some tissues. 'We'll give you some time to get dressed.' Without waiting for an answer, he walked out of the room.

'Back in a sec, Brenda.' Kate followed him into the small office next door to the kitchen, away from prying eyes.

'It didn't feel like a cyst, did it?' She knew from his expression.

'I felt a solid mass bigger than five centimetres. There's every chance it's ovarian cancer.' His hands curled into a fist. 'I want to evacuate her today, now, for tests at the base hospital.'

'Today?' Shock rocked through her. 'Wouldn't it be better if she went home tonight, got a bag organised and then she and Des could come together to Warragurra tomorrow?'

'No.' The word exploded from him like a shot from a gun. She started. 'It doesn't have to be this rushed.'

'It has to be today.' He spoke through clenched teeth.

Thoughts charged through her mind, colliding with each other as Kate struggled to understand his over-the-top reaction. 'But it's not likely that you can get the tests organised this quickly. Letting them come in tomorrow would give them both some time to absorb and adjust to the news.'

He spluttered. 'Adjust to the news? No one *adjusts* to cancer, Kate. She needs a CA 125 blood test, an ultrasound, a chest X-ray and a biopsy. And, damn it, she's having it all today.'

Her head spun as she tried to keep track of the conversation. 'But it might not even be cancer…'

He swore softly under his breath. 'You might want to live in fairyland, Kate, but I don't. She has all the vague symptoms that make ovarian cancer the silent killer it is. On top of that, she has a solid mass.' The veins in his neck throbbed as his voice almost growled. 'She needs surgery and chemotherapy yesterday and I'm damn well going to make sure she gets it, even if I have to take her to Sydney or Adelaide myself.'

His anger bore down on her like the wind from a cyclone— powerful and unforgiving. How did she tell him she thought he was overreacting? That if he went into that small room now, as agitated as he was, he'd terrify Brenda. 'Baden, perhaps I should tell her.'

His jaw stiffened and his eyes sparked like flint against stone. 'I'm the *only* one who can do this. I'm the only one that understands.'

Hot, searing pain slashed her. It was as if he'd struck her across the face. But at the same time warning bells screamed in her head. This wasn't the behaviour of a detached doctor about to give a patient bad news. Gut instinct forced her to move in front of the door but she had no idea if she was protecting Baden or Brenda.

He stood before her, his breath coming quickly, his eyes wide and his handsome face contorted. But with what? Pain? Anxiety? Grief?

She didn't know but every part of her knew something was very, very wrong. 'Baden, what's going on?'

He crossed his arms and rolled his eyes. 'Nothing is going on and that is the problem. Stand aside, Kate, so I can talk to my patient.'

'No. She's my patient, too.' She locked her knees against

their trembling. 'I've never seen you react like this. Not even last week when you had to organise tests for Mrs Hutton for suspected bowel cancer.' She took a deep breath and asked the question that plagued her. 'Why is this case different?'

Tension shuddered through him as he swung away from her, gripping the back of a chair so hard the metal strained. 'Ovarian cancer consumed my life for four years.'

Consumed? 'Did you work in the area in Adelaide before you came up here?'

He turned and faced her—his eyes deliciously blue but alarmingly empty.

A chill ran through her.

His face sagged, haggard with sorrow but lined with love. 'Ovarian cancer stole my wife. Annie died two years ago this month.'

She gave thanks the door was behind her, holding her up as a shaft of pain pierced her, taking her breath with it. He'd lost his soul-mate. The mother of his child.

She ached for him. Ached for Sasha. Suddenly his over-the-top reaction seemed reasonable. Shame filled her—she'd just exacerbated his pain by pushing him to tell her. 'I'm so sorry, Baden. I had no idea. I…'

He shrugged. 'I don't talk about it much.' He ran his hand across the back of his neck. 'Thanks.'

The word completely perplexed her. 'What on earth are you thanking me for? I think I just made things worse for you.'

He gave a wry smile. 'No, you stopped me from letting my personal feelings impact on a patient. You're right—if I had gone in to talk to her a couple of minutes ago I probably would have terrified her.' He pulled out his phone and handed it to her. 'I want you to ring the base and schedule all those appointments for tomorrow, just as you suggested.'

A glimmer of anxiety skated through her. 'Don't you want me to come in with you when you talk to Brenda?'

He shook his head. 'No. It's best we combine forces and not waste time. You get everything set up for tomorrow. I'll talk to Brenda and arrange for her and Des to fly in first thing in the morning.'

'Are you sure? Because—'

He shot her a look as if he could read her mind. 'I'm fine, Kate. February's just a tough month, that's all.'

She wasn't sure if she believed him or not. 'Would you and Sasha like to come to dinner tonight?' The words rushed from her mouth, the result of a half thought-out desire to help him get through a tough month. 'I'm sure Sasha would enjoy a horse ride or going in a canoe.'

His shoulders tensed and his eyes darkened with surprise, followed by an emotion she couldn't read.

'I'm sure she would. Thanks for the offer, but she's got school in the morning.'

Unexpected disappointment streaked through her. 'The weekend, then?' She bit her lip, hearing how needy she was sounding. How had an invitation to help him suddenly become more about her?

His azure gaze pierced her. 'Kate, would you have invited me to dinner half an hour ago?'

The question hit her out of left field, completely unnerving her. 'I... Well... Yes.'

His brows rose. 'I think we both know that isn't true. We're colleagues, not friends. You don't have to start treading on eggshells around me or start cooking for me. I don't need pity. We've had two years on our own and Sasha and I are just fine. Life goes on.'

He walked from the room, leaving her holding his phone,

the only part of himself he seemed willing to share with her. The ache for him and his loss suddenly turned and became part of her, its dull dragging pain trawling through her.

No wonder he'd pulled away from their kiss in her garden. He had nothing to offer her—his heart belonged to another woman.

She was just his flight nurse. Nothing more, nothing less.

She waited for the relief she should feel to fill her. She didn't want to lust after him, she knew the heartache magnetic attraction could wreak. She'd lived it with Shane.

A week ago being Baden's flight nurse had been all that she'd wanted. It had fitted in with her longing for a simple and uncomplicated life. A single life with good friends.

But he'd just returned her attempt at friendship.

Suddenly just being his colleague didn't seem enough.

Baden sat at the kitchen table surrounded by travel brochures. He'd gone to the travel agency on the way home, trying to squash the unsettled feeling that had been dogging him for the last few days. *Days without Kate in them.*

It had been a hell of a week. He'd broken the news to Brenda and Des and supported them through the tests. Brenda's results had been positive for cancer and she'd gone to Sydney for surgery to have her uterus, ovaries and Fallopian tubes removed. Kate had accompanied her and had rung to say the surgery had gone according to plan and Brenda would have her first round of chemotherapy before leaving Sydney.

The times Emily had accompanied patients south he'd hardly thought about her, but although Kate had been absent she'd actually been with him every moment of the day. Images played constantly through his mind—her chocolate-brown eyes that could go from warm and soothing to smouldering in a heartbeat, her delicious curves that had been burned into his memory and her throaty laugh that made his blood pound faster just thinking about it.

Sasha leaned over his shoulder, her arms curling around his neck. His guilt dug in. He'd been distracted all week, thinking of Kate instead of focussing on his daughter.

'I thought you said we couldn't go on a holiday until we'd been here a year?' She peered at the glossy pictures. 'Oh, Queensland?' She slid forward onto his lap and picked up the theme-park brochure.

He pointed to a tropical scene with bright-coloured umbrellas with gold tassels. 'What about Bali? Mum always wanted to go there.'

Her face took on a far-away look. 'The theme parks would be awesome.' Then she focussed and looked straight at him. 'And Seaworld is totally educational.' A familiar cajoling sound played through her voice.

He smiled at her obvious ploy. 'What about Bali this time and theme parks next?'

'I don't want to go to Bali.' Unexpected petulance crossed her face.

Surprise whizzed through him. 'But it's on the planner. The things we talked about doing with Mum.'

'But Mum isn't here.'

He hugged her close, wishing for the billionth time that Sasha could have her mother in her life in person rather than in memory.

She struggled out of his embrace and crossed her arms. 'Why do we always have to do what Mum wanted?'

Baden stiffened in shock as her words hailed down on him. His immediate response was to be the father in charge. 'We don't always do what your mother wanted.'

Sasha stilled. 'Yes, we do. We came to Warragurra because that was what Mum wanted to do.'

He gave her a squeeze. 'And you've made lots of friends and it's been great.'

She wriggled off his lap. 'Yeah, but staying in Adelaide might have been great, too. You didn't always do what Mum wanted when she was alive.' Tears of frustration pooled in her eyes as her anger bubbled up. 'I don't want to go to Bali. I want to do something that I want to do.' Turning on her heel, Sasha stormed off to her room, her door slamming hard behind her.

Hell. He pushed the brochures away and dropped his head in his hands. Puberty hormones had well and truly kicked in. How had a simple idea about a holiday exploded in his face? A ripple of indignation washed through him. She was being over-dramatic, a pubescent drama queen.

Coming to Warragurra had been set in place well before Annie had died. They'd planned it together, both agreeing that the country was the place to bring up a child. He'd promised Annie he would bring Sasha here and he had no regrets.

You didn't always do what Mum wanted when she was alive.

But Sasha's comment stuck like the barb of an arrow. She had a point, he'd give her that. Annie had been larger than life, such a powerful force in the family. It had made for heated debate and lively discussions about all sorts of things, and there *had* been plenty of times they hadn't agreed. Would he have gone to Bali for a holiday? Would that have been his first choice?

If the truth be known, he probably would have sided with Sash for the theme parks. There was something about a roller-coaster that had him hustling for the front seat every time. So why was he pushing for Bali now? It was only a holiday.

Sighing, he stood up and poured himself a glass of orange juice. Should he talk to Sasha's teacher about her moodiness? She'd just tell him it was normal developmental behaviour.

Kate's caring face floated across his mind. She had lots of

experience with the Guides so he could get some advice from her. He smiled at the thought.

You rejected her friendship, remember?

How could he have forgotten? From the moment he'd rejected her dinner invitation she'd been nothing but the perfect nurse. Gone were all the signs of fire and passion that he'd experienced when he'd held her in his arms, gone was the laughter and mischievous grin. In their place was a cool professional—competent, knowledgeable and proficient.

Which was everything he'd wanted, right? Safety in professional distance. He needed that distance from her. The night he'd kissed her he'd lost himself in her and forgotten his daughter, which had scared the hell out of him. His focus had to be on Sasha. She needed him. Needed him to be her mother and father. She needed stability. He couldn't let himself be distracted by Kate and that was why he'd rejected her invitation.

Curtly rejected it, and at the same time rejected her friendship.

Remorse nibbled at him as he stared out the window at the first stars of the night, twinkling against a pink and grey sky. As if anything had been going to happen at a family dinner. His knee-jerk reaction had changed their working dynamics. He missed the banter and the laughs. He missed how her eyes danced with devilment and teasing. Just plain missed the Kate he'd got to know.

He ran his hand through his hair. They had months ahead of them, working together, and for their patients' well-being they needed to be a team. He wanted his friendly colleague back, rather than the starched version. And the only way that would happen was if he apologised and offered friendship. He could do friendship. Friendship was safe, simple and straightforward. Friendship wouldn't affect Sasha.

Contentment wove through him. He'd apologise the next time he saw Kate.

But first he had to go and hug his daughter and tell her he loved her. Perhaps he could trade off theme parks with a few days of bushwalking in the hinterland. He'd give it some thought.

CHAPTER SIX

'GOODNIGHT, Koala.' Erin waved enthusiastically as she ran backwards towards the car.

'Tonight was great. Thanks heaps.' Phoebe's eyes shone with delight as she slung her bag over her shoulder.

'I'm glad you had a good time. See you next week.' Kate stood on her veranda smiling, waving and saying her good-nights to the Guides as car doors slammed, tyres crunched on the long gravel drive and young voices called their final fare-wells from open car windows.

She'd held a special Guide meeting at Sandon. They'd lit a campfire, made damper, toasted marshmallows and had had the best fun swinging from a rope and cannonballing into the water-hole. Two new girls had visited and she was confident they'd join. Word was spreading through Warragurra Public School that Guides was fun.

She closed the front door and walked back through the house to the kitchen, checking her watch. One Guide remained to be collected. One parent was late.

Sasha sat cross-legged on the floor, cuddling a black kitten that squirmed in her arms, his white feet trying to get purchase so he could make a quick exit.

'He's so cute, Kate. What's his name?'

Sasha's bright eyes and animated gaze reminded Kate of a younger version of herself. 'I've called him Snowy.'

'But he's more black than white.' She wrinkled her nose in thought and then laughed. 'Oh, I get it. That's the sort of dumb joke Dad would make.' She immediately slapped her hand over her mouth. 'Sorry, I didn't mean you were dumb.'

Kate laughed. 'That's OK. It's a silly joke but it made me smile, and the day I got Snowy I needed a smile.'

'Why?' Sasha scratched the kitten behind the ears and he stilled.

'I'd had a bad day at work. A lady got some bad news. Sometimes bad things happen to good people and it makes no sense.'

'Yeah.' Sahsa fell quiet for a bit. 'That happened to my mum. She died of cancer when I was in grade four.' Sasha buried her face in Snowy's fur.

Kate's heart bled a little for the young girl. 'That sucks.'

Sasha raised her head, her eyes wide. 'Yeah, it does.' She hugged the kitten close.

'You must miss her.'

Sadness tinged with guilt streaked across her face.

'I do miss her, but I…' Her voice trailed away, her expression uncertain.

Kate sensed she wanted to talk. 'It's OK. You can say what you feel here. It's just me and Snowy.'

'And the horses, the chickens and the dog.' Sasha waved to Rupert, the golden retriever, who stood by the French doors, looking suitably hangdog at not being allowed in the house while that upstart kitten got all the attention.

'Sure, but they've all signed the secrecy act.' Kate smiled, hoping to relax her.

Sasha hesitated and then words poured out. 'Everyone says

I must miss Mum and I really do, but it's not every day.' She gazed at Kate imploringly. 'Some days I even sometimes forget until I go to bed. Is that a bad thing? I feel really bad saying it.'

Kate put her arm around Sasha's shoulders. 'That's a normal and healthy way to feel. Mum wouldn't want you to be missing her every moment of your life. She would want you to grow up, be happy, have adventures and have fun.' *That's what I'd want for my child.*

'I miss her on my birthday and at weird times like last week when we got into the tennis finals.' Sasha blinked rapidly. 'I wanted to tell her so bad that it hurt here.' She put her hand on her chest and sighed. 'But other times I feel bad when I'm having heaps of fun. Like tonight, it was way cool swinging out over the river and letting go of that rope. Mum probably wouldn't have even let me do that! She was pretty strict sometimes.'

Kate smiled and gave her a quick squeeze. 'I think she might have let you do it now you're twelve and have passed swimming survival.' She tightened her sarong and stood up. 'I'm going to make myself an iced coffee. Would you like one of my special ice-cream milkshakes? They always make me feel better about things.'

'Yes, please.' Sasha scrambled to her feet, letting the kitten escape.

'Chocolate, caramel, strawberry or blue heaven?'

'Wow, you have all those flavours?' Disbelief shone from her face.

'Yes, I do. Pretty wicked, isn't it? But why leave behind the great things about being a kid when you grow up?' Laughing, she walked to the kitchen and pulled the blender out of the cupboard.

Sasha sat in the tall chair at the breakfast bar and tapped the top of each bottle of topping trying to decide which one to have.

An idea started to gel in Kate's mind as she mixed the drinks.

'Sasha, you know how we talked about Guide challenges last week and working toward your Junior BP award?'

Sasha nodded. 'I was thinking about doing hiking and camping for one. Once I walked from home to Ledger's Gorge. I really liked it there—it was a good place to think, you know?'

Kate understood completely. 'We all need a place to think when things are tough.'

'Yeah, and sometimes I just need to think.' Sasha seemed to shake herself and she grinned at Kate. 'But I have to do two things off the list, right?'

'You do. Hiking and camping is a fantastic choice for part one. I was thinking what if you chose service as the second topic and you helped raise some money for research into finding a test that can detect ovarian cancer early. That way you're doing something really important and something your mum would be really proud of. It could be your special thing and I'm sure the other Guides would be keen to help. We could wash cars, sell chocolates, that sort of thing.'

Sasha's eyes might be the same colour as her mother's but they sparkled just like Baden's. 'What about a drive-in-movie night like they had in the olden days? That would be so cool.'

Kate chuckled at the 'olden days.' She could remember going to a drive-in herself as a kid. But the idea was a good one. She never ceased to be amazed at the inventiveness of her Guides. Adults needed to remember the enthusiasm of youth and really listen.

She pulled open the freezer and hauled out a large container of ice cream. 'That's a sensational idea. A huge idea in fact. All the Guides could do it as part of their service badge and we could get more help from other organisations. There are plenty of wide-open spaces in Warragurra for a one-night drive-in and I'm sure we can do a joint venture with the hospital and get some publicity. I think we could get it all up and running and do it in two and a half months' time.'

Sasha beamed. 'Erin and I will write down a list of movies that might be good and—'

Rupert started barking as the doorbell chimed. 'Dad's here.' Sasha rose to her feet and raced to the door with Snowy bounding after her.

Baden. Kate's stomach flipped. *Don't do that. We've talked about this.* But talking sternly to her body made scant difference. It betrayed her every time with shimmers of delicious anticipation.

She hadn't seen him for a week as she'd been in Sydney with Brenda. Her reaction was ridiculous, considering the tension-filled few days after Brenda's diagnosis. He was only coming to collect his daughter. He wouldn't be staying; he'd been quite clear about *not* wanting to come for dinner. Not wanting to be friends.

And, really, it was for the best. She wanted an uncomplicated life after the horror of the last couple of years.

She breathed in deeply, steadying her pounding heart, and walked down the long hall. A cacophony of sound assaulted her as she reached the open front door.

Baden stood on her doorstep, his black curls damp and tight as if he'd just stepped out of the shower. His gleaming tanned skin seemed even more golden against his predominantly white open-necked shirt decorated with purple, green and pink stripes. *Sasha chose that shirt.* The thought bounced through her head as she took in the brown leather belt hugging his narrow waist and the long, pleated grey shorts sitting flat against a toned abdomen. Betraying heat quivered inside her. How did he always manage to look so good?

Rupert raced around Sasha and Baden's legs, barking as Snowy meowed frantically and climbed up Baden's shorts.

Kate tried not to laugh as Baden's arm chased a scared kitten across the back of his leg, almost tap-dancing at the same time.

Sasha, oblivious to her father's ripping skin, danced up and down and talked excitedly. 'Dad, this place is so cool and that's Snowy, he's new, and that's Rupert, and he's not new. Sit, Rupert.' Sasha's stern voice surprised the dog, who obediently sat but kept his eye fixed on the kitten. 'And I learned how to light a fire plus we're going to have a drive-in for money for a test for cancer like Mum's and—'

'Whoa, there, Sash.' Baden raised one hand while the other one finally gripped the kitten around the scruff of its neck. Love and laughter shone from his eyes. 'That all sounds fantastic, but how about one bit of news at a time for your poor old dad?' He glanced over the top of Sasha's head, catching sight of Kate. His dancing eyes faded to serious.

Her stomach dropped at the change in his demeanour.

'Sorry I'm late.'

Kate swallowed hard. 'That's OK. The others only left fifteen minutes ago and Sasha and I were getting to know each other.' She bit her lip. 'Sorry about the kitten using you as a climbing post.'

He gave a wry smile as he clamped the squirming kitten with one large hand and scratched Rupert behind the ear with the other. 'Cats love me. Personally, I'm siding with the dog.'

'Dad, Kate's making me a milkshake so can I stay and have mine? Please?' She slid her hand into Baden's. 'You can have one, too.' She immediately swung back to Kate. 'I mean, if that's OK.'

Kate saw a ripple of tension race across Baden's shoulders, and the residual stiffness that remained. It matched his taken-aback look. Steeling herself for his polite refusal, she opened her mouth to confirm Sasha's invitation but Baden spoke first.

'How does that suit you, Kate?' Electric blue eyes questioned her. 'Would we be imposing if we stayed for milkshakes?'

Astonishment burst through her, making her giddy. 'That would be fine.'

'Dad, she's got blue heaven!'

'Has she, now?' He winked at Sasha and then turned to face Kate, his face relaxing into a devastating smile. 'In that case, we have to stay.'

Suddenly an innocuous invitation took on dangerous undertones. The serious, aloof Baden was so much easier to resist.

Baden watched pure ecstasy race across his daughter's face as she sat outside at Kate's large wooden table, sipping a blue heaven milkshake with whipped cream and a cherry on top.

They'd spent an enjoyable and relaxed half-hour making and drinking milkshakes along with a lot of talking, laughter and teasing. Sasha, who could be quiet with adults, was a veritable chatterbox with Kate. Her animated face glowed and her eyes shone when she talked about the fundraising idea of the drive-in.

Kate treated her as a young woman rather than a little girl, asking her opinion on a range of things and gently steering her enthusiasm into achievable ideas. Baden had a sneaking suspicion that the idea of raising funds for ovarian cancer research was Kate's idea but it was a great idea and would help Sasha feel more connected to her mother's memory.

But most of all he loved the fact his daughter was having so much fun.

'This was such a random idea.' Sasha used her long spoon to get the froth from the bottom of the glass.

Baden laughed. 'That's the ultimate compliment, Kate.'

Her lips curved into a soft, enticing smile. 'If I hear random or awesome, I know I'm on the right track.'

Rupert trotted over, a large stick in his mouth, and gazed up at Sasha.

'Can I go and play with him?' She half rose as she asked the question.

Baden checked the time. 'Just for a bit—we have to leave soon. Oh, and put on some insect repellent. The sun's setting and the mosquitoes are coming out. You don't want to get Ross River fever.'

Sasha rolled her eyes. 'Da-ad.'

Kate casually reached behind her to a trolley and picked up the repellent and some matches. She handed the roll-on to Sasha and the matches to Baden. 'You put on the roll-on and your father can light the citronella flares and then we're all protected.'

'Deal.' Sasha grinned. 'Come on, Dad, on with the job.'

'Cheeky!' He grabbed his daughter, tickling her.

Delighted shrieks rose in the air before she managed to escape his grasp and run off with the roll-on, with Rupert racing after her, his golden coat flying.

Baden lit the citronella candles as instructed, thinking about what had just happened. In the most casual way Kate had just deflected a potential standoff between him and Sasha. In fact it had turned into one of those special moments of fun with Sasha that he treasured so much.

He turned back to see Kate sitting in the fading light. The rays of the setting sun danced across her face, highlighting the honey streaks in her hair, the way her soft skin stretched across her high cheekbones and the plump lushness of her mouth. Her laughing eyes caught his.

A jolt of heat flared deep inside him. He returned the matches to the trolley, wishing he could extinguish his reaction to Kate as easily as blowing out the match.

Kate's gaze followed Sasha and the dog across the lawn. 'You have a lovely daughter, Baden.'

Pride filled him. 'Thanks. I think so. Well, most of the time anyway.' He sat down next to her.

'That's pretty much representative of all of us, isn't it?' She rested back in her wide cane chair, all long-legged gracefulness.

His gaze centred in on the toned expanse of skin that the fall of the sarong exposed. *You came in to apologise, so get on with it.* His brain pulled his attention back to the job in hand.

'You're right.' He cleared his throat against a husky voice. 'Last week I had a moment when I should have behaved better.'

Her sculpted brows rose slightly in question as surprise tickled her cheeks, but she remained silent.

'I was insensitive and rude to you when you invited Sasha and me over to dinner. I want to apologise for that.'

She shrugged. 'February is your tough month. We all have to get through things in our own way and not everyone wants company. I understand that.'

She said it as if it was common knowledge but he knew so many people didn't get it. Well-meaning friends had almost smothered him when Annie had died. He hooked her gaze. 'Yes, but you were trying to be a supportive colleague and instead of responding to that I threw your good intentions and your friendship back in your face. I completely overreacted to a simple invitation for a meal.'

Intelligent brown eyes looked straight at him, seeing clear down to his soul. 'You don't have to worry about me chasing you, you know.'

Her candour hit him in the chest. She'd pegged him so accurately it was as if she was in his head, reading his thoughts. Knowing that he feared she might expect more after that kiss. Knowing he couldn't give it.

She continued, a wry smile tugging at her lips. 'After the last few years I'm not in the market for any sort of relationship and I doubt you are either. But I'd like to think we can be friends.'

He grinned as a sensation of lightness streaked through him. 'Friends would be good.' The delight of shared understanding flowed through him. 'Your insight's pretty spot on. Sasha is my top priority now and I'm flat out just keeping up with being a doctor and a father.'

She nodded slowly, her previous expression evolving into a gentle, warm smile, which raced to her eyes. 'You're doing a great job on both fronts.'

He wanted to take her praise and hold it close but a nagging truth spoke up. 'The doctoring compliment I'll accept.' He sighed. 'The parenting, well, I'm not so sure. Sasha hasn't had the uncomplicated childhood that a parent hopes for. Annie's illness was tough on her.'

'It would have been tough on you both.'

Her quiet words circled him with understanding, calling to him, relaxing him. 'The only thing cancer gives you is a chance to tie up all the loose ends, say all the things you ever wanted to say to the person who is dying. Annie and I had been together since high school. We knew each other so well that sometimes we'd finish each other's thoughts and sentences.'

He frowned, remembering some of their arguments. 'Other times we weren't so in tune with each other, but at the end we were both able to put our disagreements aside, say what needed to be said and plan for what would be best for Sasha.

'But cancer steals away everything else.' He shifted in his seat and sighed. 'It stole Sasha's mother. Sash still has all those "firsts" ahead of her and her mum won't be there to help her celebrate them.'

She reached out and touched his hand with the briefest

caress, her warmth spreading through him, almost intoxicating. A chill immediately followed when her fingers left his skin. 'But her father will be there to celebrate.'

His fears for Sasha rose to the surface, almost choking him. 'But will it be enough?' He ran his hand through his hair. 'I'm trying to help her by keeping things the same as they would have been if her mother was still alive.'

Kate tilted her head, confusion creasing her brow. 'How can you do that when her mother has died and everything has changed?'

He shrugged. 'It's not that hard. I've just continued with the family five-year plan.'

She blinked rapidly, as if trying to absorb his statement. 'And that involved leaving extended family and coming to Warragurra, even though your circumstances had changed so much?'

A niggle of annoyance zipped through him at her lack of understanding. 'That's right. It was important to stick to the plan.'

'Really?' Scepticism sounded in her voice. 'You know, Sasha strikes me as pretty mature for her age. I think she's more resilient than you give her credit for.'

Ire simmered inside him. Kate didn't know Sasha like he did. 'She's settled because we've stuck with the plan.' He heard the defensive note in his voice. 'Coming here was important for Sasha because it was what her mother wanted.'

'I think perhaps coming here was important for you. It gave you a map in uncertain times.'

Her words punched him hard, taking the air from his lungs, making his head spin. *Important for you*. His brain railed at the thought. No, she was wrong! Everything he did, he did with Sasha first and foremost in his mind. She always came first.

Resentment surged through him, breaking out against his

imposed control. 'Coming here was a considered decision. I'm not so grief-stricken that I'm blindly following a path.'

'I didn't say you were.'

Her calm tone infuriated him but at the same time it released unexpected feelings, which swirled inside him in a maelstrom of indignation. 'I could have worked anywhere but kids need stability and that's what I'm giving Sasha. She misses her mother and I'm trying to make things as easy and as uncomplicated as possible for her.'

Wide eyes as lush and rich as melted chocolate stared back at him. Understanding tangoed with disagreement.

She bit her lip. 'We can't protect the people we love from everything, no matter how much we want to. Sometimes sheltering them too much is the worst thing we can do.'

He wanted to say *What do you know?* and ignore her comment, but experience showed in the lines around her eyes. He knew then she was thinking of her husband and his parents.

'I'm *not* sheltering Sasha.' He grabbed a calming breath and dropped his voice. 'I'm doing what's best for her. She's lost her mother so doing things her mother wanted for her is the next best thing.' He waited for Kate's response, to hear her agreement. For some ridiculous reason he needed her to say he was doing the right thing.

But her expression, which up until then had mirrored her thoughts, smoothed into neutral, doing little to reassure him.

'Dad, Kate, grab the frisbee off Rupert before he gets to the hedge,' Sasha's breathless voice called as the dog raced toward them.

Laughing, Kate rose to her feet and started to run, her long legs quickly eating up the distance. She threw herself at the animal, rolling onto the lawn, her arms full of dog, her face full of joy.

Devastating loneliness pounded him, leaving behind an aching longing. He wanted to be part of that joy. Hell, he wanted to be in her arms. But that wasn't part of his plan. She didn't want a relationship and he had a daughter to care for.

Make Sasha your top priority. He had a promise to keep and a relationship would take his attention from Sasha. His focus couldn't waver from Sasha. He and Sasha were a team with a plan and he was doing what was best for them both. He was an adult and he knew best, no matter what his daughter said or a childless colleague with eyes that he could sink into and a body that he longed to hold against his own.

His plan was right. It had to be right. He squashed the tiny seed of doubt that had raised its head.

CHAPTER SEVEN

THE hospital lift opened at the second floor and Kate stepped out, immediately turning left. The antiseptic smell mixing with the aromas of the evening meal met her at the ward door and instantly took her back four years to when she had worked here.

She walked to ward 7E and knocked as she pushed the door half-open. 'Brenda, it's Kate.'

A tired voice answered. 'Come in, Kate.'

It had been two months since Brenda had gone to Sydney for surgery. Kate quietly closed the door behind her and sat down in the chair next to the bed. 'I heard you were in for a visit so I thought I'd pop in and say hi.'

Brenda gave a weary smile. 'That's kind of you, Kate. Visiting sick people after a day of working with them isn't exactly R & R for you.'

Kate gave Brenda's hand a gentle squeeze and caught sight of a bright red turban hanging on one hook of the IV stand. The chemotherapy cocktail of drugs hung on the other. 'How's the chemo going?'

'Fine. This is my third cycle and boy, those three weeks between treatments fly past.' She gave a resigned sigh. 'I'm halfway—three down and three to go. The first was the worst because I had no idea what to expect, but now I know about the nausea. As long as I take the antiemetics at the right time I can keep it under control.'

She ran her hand over her head. 'And I haven't got any hair left to lose so that's one less thing to worry about. You have no idea how much time I save in the mornings now I don't have to dry it.' Her dry humour radiated through the words.

Kate tried to smile as sadness settled in her belly. Brenda's no-nonsense approach to life extended to battling a really tough illness. Stage-two cancer was no walk in the park. 'Are you eating enough? You're looking pretty thin.'

Brenda nestled back onto a bank of pillows. 'I eat when I feel like eating. The hospital food isn't always what I want.'

'Can I get you something or make you something you'd enjoy? I make a terrific rice soup and I could whip up a batch tonight for you.' Cooking was the least she could do to help, and she wished she'd thought of it sooner.

'That's kind but—'

A knock sounded on the door. 'Ta-dah! Your take-away order has arrived.' Baden walked into the room, clutching two plastic food containers.

A flush of warmth spread through Kate at his thoughtful gesture. She finished Brenda's sentence for her. 'But Baden has already cooked for you, I see.'

He grinned as he put the food down. 'I wish. But although my chicken soup is good, there's nothing like Walter Wong's chicken and sweetcorn wonton soup for feeding body and soul.' He produced a wide, flat Chinese spoon. 'Eat it while it's hot, Brenda.'

Anticipated delight played across the sick woman's face. 'It smells so good. Thanks for thinking of me, Baden. Des usually brings it in but he had to go home and feed the stock.'

'My pleasure.' He caught Kate's gaze.

She knew immediately he was thinking that compared to what Brenda was facing, him buying some soup was a minuscule effort. But not everyone would have thought of it and that was what made it so special to Brenda.

And to you. The familiar voice chimed in her head. Not every doctor would do something like that. Not every man.

Baden picked up the chart.

Kate chuckled. 'You just can't help yourself, can you?'

He shot her a guilty look. 'Just checking to see that the oncologist is on the money.' His eyes darkened and his expression became serious. 'Brenda, make sure the nurses give you the dexamethasone on time.'

'Yes, Doctor.' Brenda gave him a mock salute with the plastic spoon.

He laughed. 'OK, so while I'm being bossy I'll add one more thing. Sleep. As soon as you've finished that soup then sleep so you can enjoy Des's visit tomorrow. Kate and I will leave you in peace but we'll see you in two weeks at the Gemton clinic between chemo courses.'

Brenda put down her spoon and reached out a hand to touch them both. 'You're both doing too much, but thank you anyway.'

'Glad to help.' Baden's voice sounded unusually gruff.

Kate breathed in deeply, feeling unworthy of her thanks. 'I'll look forward to seeing you in one of your bright coloured turbans when we catch up in Gemton.'

'I'll see you both before Gemton. I'm coming to the drive-in night and I'm bringing the entire family, including the cousins who are flying in from Dubbo. All the women are going to wear teal green turbans—it's the worldwide colour to represent ovarian cancer.'

'That sounds fantastic.' Kate marvelled at Brenda's strength.

'Baden explained to me how the CA 125 test can give false

positives.' She shrugged. 'In my case it wasn't a false result but no woman needs the stress of thinking she has cancer when she really has fibroids or endometriosis.' Brenda started waving her spoon. 'Every woman deserves to have a test that is going to be accurate for this disease and I plan to push this cause for as long as I have breath in me.'

She laughed. 'That's enough on the soapbox. Right, off you both go, my soup will get cold.' Brenda shooed them away with one hand and dipped the spoon into the soup with the other.

Kate felt Baden's arm lightly circle her waist to guide her out of the room. Automatically, every particle of her tried to flatten itself against the contact, absorbing as much of his touch as possible. *You're so weak, Kate.*

Guiltily, she stomped on the voice, knowing it to be true, and once out in the corridor she stepped forward, breaking the contact. She put on a no-nonsense voice to cover her lapse. 'I didn't realise you were calling in.'

He shrugged. 'I wasn't, but Sasha got an unexpected invitation for a pizza and movie night so I thought I'd drop by. What about you?'

'Oh, I didn't have any plans so I called in on my way home.' She didn't want to admit that the house was far too quiet, even with Snowy and Rupert.

He shoved his hands in his pockets, his eyes suddenly twinkling against his dark five o'clock shadow—the incredibly sexy pirate look. 'We're both pretty pathetic, then, aren't we? It's Friday night and we're standing in a hospital with empty houses to go to. How about we grab some dinner together? That gives us three hours before I have to pick Sasha up at ten.'

'Sounds like a plan.' Since their conversation at her place they'd settled into a comfortable friendship. Well, comfortable on his side. He treated her like a mate and they talked about all sorts of things. But she still had this crazy super-awareness of him, which had her spinning in circles. His casual touches when he opened doors or moved past her made her dizzy with longing, and she ached with a growing need she'd never experienced before.

But nothing could come of it and she had to learn to control it. Friendship was all she wanted.

Liar.

She refused to listen to the traitorous voice in her head that grew louder daily and played havoc with her dreams at night. 'So where shall we go?'

Baden pressed the 'down' button on the lift. 'The Royal Hotel is the closest and Jen raved about the beef she had there the other night.'

The Kennedy hotel. Fear clawed her. Bile burned her throat and her heart pounded so fast she thought it would bound out of her chest. 'I can't go to the Royal.'

He spoke quietly. 'Can't or won't? There's a difference.'

She struggled to think against her rising panic. 'You know why I can't go there.' His betrayal fizzed in her veins. 'I can't believe you would even suggest it.'

The light above the lift lit up and the 'ping' sounded as the doors opened. Wrapping her arms tightly around her, Kate stepped into the empty silver box. Anger started to overtake the panic as she punched the ground-floor button.

Baden followed. 'Kate, you live in this town and you have the right to dine where you choose. It's the best restaurant in Warragurra. It just won three hats for country cuisine and I want to take you there so you can enjoy the food.'

She shook her head in disbelief. 'You don't get it, do you? Shane's family owns part of that hotel.'

He stood tall and implacable. 'You can't hide out for the rest of your life, Kate.'

'But if I go there it's as if I'm thumbing my nose at Shane's family's pain.' The lift opened and she stormed out, walking as fast as she could without running.

'Kate.'

She heard his plea for her to slow down but she kept walking.

His hand caught hers and he gently steered her into an interview room and closed the door. 'Let's talk about this.'

Furious with him, she shook his hand away. Immediately the fury turned back against her as the loss of contact throbbed through her like a dull ache. She hadn't wanted to let go. She'd wanted to grip on to his hand tightly, using it like a life raft in a stormy sea.

Baden raked his hand through his hair. 'Don't you think it's time to stop taking the blame for something that wasn't your fault? You're letting Shane's parents' grief control your life. Hiding out won't solve the problem.'

'I'm not hiding out.' How dare he accuse her of that? 'I'm here, back in town, running Guides and—'

'Avoiding this part of town.' He stepped in closer.

His heat washed over her, diluting her anger. 'I don't want to push this. Shane's parents need time.'

'They've had over a year already. You're a lovely person, Kate. Anyone who truly knows you will realise that it's grief that's making the Kennedys act so irrationally.'

'Yes, but—'

'No buts. You need to be seen in town. We have this big fundraiser for the ovarian cancer predictive test research coming up. You've put in hours getting the hospital on board, the flyers printed, you've liaised with the school and you've brokered a deal with the movie-hire company. I haven't even mentioned the diplomatic juggling act of getting five social service groups to work together with the Guides for the fete and food stall side of the night. It's bigger than big.'

Warmth filled her at his praise.

He continued, his face serious. 'The Kennedys and their rich and influential friends need to know what you're doing. They need to know that most of the people in this town respect you enough to back this project. Having them on board will only help ovarian cancer research.'

'So you just want me to do this for fundraising purposes, irrespective of my feelings?' Anger and dread swirled together in the pit of her stomach, forcing nausea to rise. She couldn't believe he was so blinkered that he would put his own feelings ahead of hers.

He shook his head, his eyes dark with thought. 'No, I want to do this for you. If you walk into the pub with me tonight, we're a united front. We're showing people that time has moved on.'

I want to do this for you. His thoughtfulness scared her almost as much as walking into the Royal. No one had done anything like this for her. Sure, she'd had lots of support from people out of town but no one in town had offered such solidarity.

He kept talking, ignoring her silence. 'I've already spoken to the manager and he's happily put up a poster for the drive-in and has flyers on the bar tables. You'd be welcome. You can do this. I know it's a big step but it's a step you have to take.'

A thousand thoughts zipped through her mind, colliding and jumbling as she tried to think past her panic. She hated it that he was right.

Baden's arm touched hers. She looked into the clearest of clear blue eyes. Eyes that held understanding and determination. 'If you won't do it for yourself then do if for Brenda and other women like her.'

Like Sasha's mother.

Sasha had lost her mother. Baden had lost his wife to this

silent killer. All she had to do was face down a crowd, and perhaps not even that. She breathed in deeply and bit her lip. 'You'll be there all the time?'

He smiled, his face creasing in familiar lines. 'Right beside you.'

Tendrils of longing winged through her, flattening her fear. With Baden next to her she could do this. 'If Brenda can face down cancer and chemo and still crack jokes then I guess I can face down the Kennedys.'

'Fantastic. Let's go.' He reached for her hand.

She spun out of his reach. 'I'll dine at the Royal on two conditions.'

He raised his dark brows in silent question.

'I'm having the seafood platter and you're paying.'

He laughed, the sound so deep it vibrated in her chest.

'What, no dessert?'

She grinned. 'Oh, good idea. I hear their lemon pie is a must.'

He stepped in close, his hands lightly touching her shoulders and slowly trailing down her arms until his hands held hers.

Her mind blanked at his touch.

For a moment she thought she saw desire sparkling in his eyes like sunlight on water, but when she looked again she could only see humour.

He spoke softly, his voice husky with laughter. 'You drive a hard bargain, Kate Lawson. Have you been taking lessons from Sasha?'

'Us girls have to stick together, you know.' Girly giggles bubbled up on a trail of sheer lightness and joy. It took her a moment to recognise the sensation. Happiness. It had been a long time since she'd felt like this…if she'd ever really felt like this.

'Come on, then, before I change my mind or you add French champagne into the mix.'

'That would be an idea if I drank, but I'll happily have French mineral water.'

He pulled her toward the door and out onto the street, their laughter filling the early evening air.

'Race you.' He dropped her hand and started jogging down the street, quickly turning a corner with a wicked wave.

'Hey!' Surprise stalled her for a moment before she began to run, giving thanks she was still in her flat work shoes. She caught him up at the steps of the Royal.

He was leaning casually against the highly polished brass banister, his face devastatingly handsome. 'What kept you?'

She panted indignantly and slugged him playfully on the arm. 'That was cheating. I'm sure I deserved a handicap start.'

He caught her elbow and steered her up the stairs, his head close to hers. 'You're here now, though.' The soft words caressed her hair, her ear and all the way down to her toes.

Realisation slammed through her. He'd used the race to distract her so she wouldn't start to stress on the short walk. She bit her lip. His brand of friendship was everything anyone could want. *Except you want more.*

She tossed the treacherous thought away.

His arm touched the small of her back as he ushered her through the door. As he joined her at the maître d's lectern, his arm circled her waist, the pressure reassuring.

Her heart pounded as she glanced into the dining room but all she could see was a sea of heads.

'Just walk. I'm right here.' Baden gently pushed her forward as the maître d' led the way to their table.

She stared straight ahead, her sight blurred and her mouth dry. Why had she let him talk her into this? Was she such a fool for sky-blue eyes that she'd agree to anything?

In a flurry of scraping chairs and white napkins, Kate found herself sitting opposite Baden, staring hard at the menu.

'I thought you knew what you were having. You can look up, you know.'

His cheeky tone made her lower the tall menu. 'It's all right for you, you're not about to be lynched.'

A serious look streaked through his eyes. 'Neither are you.'

She glanced around. She recognised a few faces. Some tilted their heads to acknowledge her. She forced a returning smile.

Baden ordered and the waiter returned with mineral water, nutcrackers for the lobster legs and hot bread rolls. Kate used every ounce of willpower not to down the glass of water in one go. Instead, she mangled a bread roll.

'Dr Tremont, Katie.'

She looked up to see Richie Santini standing next to their table, holding a glass of mineral water.

Baden rose to his feet and shook Richie's extended hand.

She swallowed hard and tried to sound relaxed. 'Hello, Richie. You're looking better than when I saw you last.'

'That wouldn't be hard, would it?' The man grimaced. 'I saw you come in and I just wanted to say…'

Kate flinched, waiting for the expected words of hatred to follow.

Richie cleared his throat. 'I just wanted to say thanks. They told me at the hospital that without the two of you doing CPR, I wouldn't be here.'

Incredulity stole her breath.

'We're just glad we were there, aren't we, Kate?' Baden's voice filled the gap as he tilted his head encouragingly, his gaze saying *It's your turn to speak.*

She nodded, desperately trying to find her voice against a tight throat filled with emotion. 'It's good to see you, Richie.'

She clinked her glass of water against his, acknowledging the fact he wasn't drinking alcohol.

'Yeah. I'm off the grog. Josh is trying it, too. He's gone to Adelaide for a bit to a clinic there. The Kennedys are paying him sick leave and the cost of the rehab.' He shifted his weight from one foot to the other. 'Turns out you were right after all, Katie. We've been drinking too much for years.'

A rush of thankfulness filled her. At least two of Shane's friends had a second chance. 'It's not about being right, Richie. I'm just glad both of you are getting some help.'

He nodded, his expression resigned. 'I'll see you at that drive-in night, then. Enjoy your meal.' He walked away to his table.

'I can't believe that just happened. And Josh…' She shook her head, bewildered by the thought that Josh was in rehab and that Shane's parents were funding it.

Baden's lips curved into a self-satisfied smile. 'I told you that coming here wouldn't be a bad experience.' He raised his glass. 'To your future in Warragurra.'

My future. She should be thrilled that the town was thawing, and on one level she was. On another level she peered into the future and saw only herself. It looked lonelier than it had a few weeks ago.

As she raised her glass to his, the seafood platter arrived at the table. Laden with crayfish, prawns, oysters and Moreton Bay bugs, the table almost groaned under the weight.

The waiter proceeded to clip a bib around each of them. 'Enjoy it. It's absolutely fresh, flown in from the coast this morning.'

'I feel like I'm at the dentist.' Kate chuckled at the white paper bib.

'I'm hoping dinner will be a more enjoyable experience.' Baden smiled his devilish smile as he cracked open a crayfish leg. 'It's not an elegant meal, that's for sure.'

They laughed their way through sensational food, sticky fingers, dribbles down chins and stray squirts of liquid as they cracked, peeled and shucked seafood. They covered a wide variety of topics and never once talked about work. Kate couldn't remember the last time she'd had so much fun.

As she washed her fingers in the lemon-scented water provided for the purpose, she caught sight of Hilary Smithton, bearing down on their table like a rhinoceros at full charge.

The wonderful food curdled in her stomach. She tried for the upper hand. 'Hello, Hilary.'

The seething woman laid her hands palms down on the table, her eyes glittering with anger. 'You've got a hide, coming in here, Kate. Shane made the biggest mistake of his life choosing you over me.' Her voice cracked. 'If he'd married me, he'd still be here.'

And suddenly the years of vitriol all fell into place. Hilary had loved Shane. She blinked rapidly against the futility of hatred. Instinctively she reached out to touch Hilary's hand, to acknowledge that she, too, had lost something, someone.

Hilary pulled her hand away as if the touch had scalded her. 'You might be duping everyone with your saintly fundraising act but I'm not falling for it.'

Baden leaned back casually in his chair, a pleasant smile on his face, but Kate caught an unusual steely glint in his sparkling eyes.

Hilary barely flicked him a glance, her concentration one hundred per cent on Kate. Her lips thinned. 'I won't be coming to your drive-in night and Lucy won't be part of the night either.'

'That's your choice, Hilary, although sad for Lucy.' Kate kept her voice even.

'Good luck with that.' Baden's smooth, controlled voice chimed in, his tone sceptical. 'I know I wouldn't want to be the parent who had to break the news to their kid that they would be the *only* senior student at Warragurra Public School not involved in making fairy floss, cooking sausages or selling smoothies at the drive-in.'

Disconcerted, Hilary swung around to face him. 'What are you on about? It's just the Guides.'

Baden shook his head. 'No, Hilary, it's the town. The town has taken on this project. The hospital is backing it and the school is making it the social service activity of the term. Sure, the Guides are involved, but it's much, much bigger than the Guides. It's bigger than any single person with a personal beef. Every person in this town who has a mother or sister or daughter wants to see a screening test for ovarian cancer become a reality. They're backing the research with their time, money and support.'

All colour faded from Hilary's face before surging back, her cheeks turning bright red. 'Don't preach to me, Dr Tremont. I have the right to choose my own causes.' She spun away from the table and walked out the door.

Baden's words resonated in Kate's head. Was *this* what it was like to be cared for? He had this knack of making her feel special…cherished. *Your mind is running away from you. The fundraising is special to him, too.* Of course it was.

He grinned at Kate, his eyes dancing with wickedness and his curls bouncing with laughter. 'Well, you can't have the whole town liking you, Kate.'

'No, that wouldn't seem right, would it? Hilary will keep me very grounded.' She ran her fingers around the edge of the linen napkin. 'I feel sorry for her, though. She lost Shane twice. Once to me and once to death.'

'But you lost him twice, too. Once to alcohol and once to death.' His quiet voice seemed to caress her.

'I guess I did. It sounds an awful thing to say but I think her loss is greater than mine. Shane is my past and now I'm only looking forward. I've moved on.'

'Have you?' His serious gaze penetrated deeply, as if exposing all her feelings.

'I have.' She caught a shudder of tension ripple through him. 'And what about you?' The words left her mouth on a jet of need before her brain had the sense to cut them off.

His jaw stiffened and his eyes darkened to unreadable before his gaze slid to his watch.

A chill raced through her. Why had she asked? Had she thought if she asked the question it would give her a different answer from the one she knew dwelt in his heart? His situation was so very different from hers. He'd lost a wife he'd loved, lost a happy marriage, a companion, a mother to his child. Of course he hadn't moved on.

She drew on every ounce of acting ability she had, looked at her own watch and jumped to her feet. 'Thanks for a lovely meal, but look at the time. You'd better not be late for Sasha.'

He immediately stood, his expression a jumble of feelings she found impossible to decode. 'Sorry. I do need to go. But it's been great.'

His bonhomie flew to her heart like a poisoned arrow. Until this moment she'd never realised that friendship could be so painful.

Baden stood on Phoebe Walton's veranda at nine-fifty p.m.

He'd hardly noticed the twenty-minute drive out to the farm— his mind had been full of Kate. He could have sat opposite her for hours, just watching the way her smile danced along her cheekbones, how her hair fell so silkily, framing her heart-shaped face, and how her long, thick eyelashes brushed her skin.

But it was the image of her lush lips that stayed with him.

Vivid memories of their touch and taste hovered so very close to the surface of every hour of every day that it terrified him.

He'd loved before and had lost everything. *Except Sasha.* He still had Sasha and she was where his priorities had to lie.

But Kate... He jabbed the doorbell viciously, driving the voice away.

Phoebe's mother, Evelyn, opened the door. 'Hi, Baden. Come in, I'll just get Sasha.'

'Thanks.' Baden stepped into the hall and admired Evelyn's artwork, which was going to be on display in the foyer of the hospital as part of the fundraising drive.

Two minutes later he heard Sasha politely thanking Phoebe's mother for having her, but when she appeared in the hall she stomped toward him, her expression grumpy. 'Dad, you're early. None of the other parents are here yet.'

He waved goodnight to Evelyn, picked up Sasha's backpack and slung his arm around her shoulder as they walked toward the car. 'I'm not that early. Mrs Walton said ten o'clock.'

'But the second movie hasn't finished.' She glanced longingly back at the closed door.

'Sorry, sweetheart, but you've got tennis in the morning.' He unlocked the car doors and they both got in.

Sasha tugged at her seat belt, jamming the latch into place with a loud click. 'It's Friday night, Dad. You should have gone out like other parents. I bet you stayed at home and got bored and that's why you're early.' She fixed him with a glare. 'You need some friends, Dad. I've got friends. You need some, too, so you're not just worrying about me all the time.'

Her words chafed at him, irritating and grating. He didn't worry about her—he just wanted what was best for her. 'As a matter of fact, I did go out.'

'What, on your own?' She slumped into the seat, all petulance and peevishness.

'No.' He had an idiotic desire to puff out his chest and boast,
proving to her he wasn't the boring old fuddy-duddy she obviously thought him. 'With Kate.'

Sasha sat up so fast her seat belt locked against her.
Incredulity shone in her eyes. 'Really?'

'Yes, really.' He grinned foolishly.

'Cool! Kate rocks.' She studied him for a minute. 'What did
you do?' Active interest radiated from her.

'We had dinner at the Royal.' The grin stayed on his face,
refusing to slide away.

'Didn't you have a nice time?'

'What sort of question is that? Of course I did. I had a great
time.' Images of the enjoyable evening rolled out in his mind.

'So why are you here early, then?'

Her penetrating stare sent guilt snaking through him.

Because I was having too much fun.

*Because I'm thinking more about Kate than about you and
your mother, and that scares me rigid.*

The love he'd had for Annie, the girl next door whom he'd
married, had never felt like this all-consuming rush he experienced with Kate. His marriage had been comforting, de-
pendable and companionable. He'd grieved for Annie but just
lately when he thought of her he didn't ache with loss. He
should still be aching. He should still be missing her as much
as Sasha missed her.

But he couldn't tell his daughter any of this.

He gently prodded Sasha in the ribs. 'Why was I early?
Because, my darling daughter, you know I'm never late.'

Sasha laughed. 'Dad, your jokes are so lame. You are
always late.'

'OK, I confess. Kate reminded me of the time so it's her fault. Next time you see her, you tell her how you missed the end of the movie.'

'As if!' Sasha rolled her eyes and turned on the CD player, finding her favourite track. 'Dad.'

'Hmm.'

'It was fun the night we made milkshakes with Kate. Do you think now you've been to dinner with her she might invite us back to Sandon again?'

He caught her wistful expression. 'I don't know, sweetheart. Perhaps.' But the rush of hope that raced through him at the thought matched Sasha's.

CHAPTER EIGHT

'KATE, I think the allergies have started early this year. I've never had headaches like it. I've even been wearing my sunglasses inside.' Debbie Grayson's colour matched her surname as she slumped in the chair at her kitchen table.

Kate and Baden had finished their clinic and were waiting for Glen to return to collect them. Baden had wandered off with Cameron, Debbie's husband, to look at the new quad bikes Cameron had bought as part of his foray into tourism on the Darling.

'That's no good. Do you want me to have a look at you?' Kate put down her cup of tea.

Debbie looked relieved. 'Would you mind? I feel like I'm taking advantage of you.'

'Don't be silly. You've hosted the day and if you're not well, it's crazy for me to leave without examining you.' She opened her bag and pulled out the ear thermometer.

'They sure beat shaking down the old mercury thermometers.' Debbie tucked her hair behind her ear in readiness.

A moment later the thermometer beeped. 'You've got a slight fever.' Kate gently palpated Debbie's glands. 'And your glands are up but that just tells us your body is fighting something. You said the headaches were different—how are they different?'

'I can't stand bright light and I feel like I've got ants crawling on my skin, around my eye and up into my scalp.' She grimaced. 'The pain is so intense sometimes I feel like crying.'

'And that's not like you at all.' Kate had known Debbie for almost as long as she'd lived in Warragurra. Debbie had been the medical records clerk in ICU at the base hospital until Cameron Grayson had swept her off her feet and brought her out to Bungarra station. Kate snapped on some gloves. 'I'm just going to look in your hair.'

'I said it felt like ants, but I don't have ants or head lice.' Debbie sounded indignant.

Kate parted Debbie's hair and saw a faint rash running along her scalp in a straight line, with occasional blisters. She peered closely at Debbie's forehead and could see a faint red line, a sign of things to come. 'Have you had any sick tourists here lately? Kids?'

Debbie frowned in thought. 'No, I don't think… Oh, yeah, a few weeks ago one poor family had to leave early because both their children came down with chickenpox. But I had chickenpox as a kid so it can't be that, thank goodness.'

Kate stripped off her gloves. 'No, but you can get shingles.'

A horrified look crossed her face. 'Shingles! But I'm only thirty-one and that's an old person's disease.'

Kate shook her head. 'Sorry. You've been flat out getting this new tourist venture up and running, and anyone who's a bit run down and who comes in contact with the herpes zoster virus can have the virus reactivated. Only this time you don't get chickenpox, you get shingles, and the virus runs along the nerve it's been hibernating in for all those years. In your case, it's running along the fifth cranial nerve.'

'So what happens now?' Debbie stared at her anxiously.

'We get Baden to confirm my diagnosis and then we start

you on antiviral medication. I'll just go and give the boys the hurry-up. They should have talked torque and RPMs and all that engine stuff by now, as well as test driven the bikes.' She walked outside and saw the men, both deep in conversation and striding back toward the house.

'Coo-ee.' She gave the bush call.

Baden immediately looked up, and gave her a wave and a smile.

A smile that sent tendrils of pleasure spiralling through her. A smile she hugged close and revisited too often on long, lonely nights.

The men increased their pace and Baden was the first to reach the bottom of the veranda steps, his long legs taking them two at a time. 'Are we ready to go?'

'No, Glen hasn't called yet. But I think Debbie has shingles.'

'What's that?' Cameron's concerned voice broke into their conversation.

'Come inside, mate, and I'll explain it to both of you at the same time.' Baden opened the wire door and ushered everyone inside.

Baden examined Debbie. 'You're lucky we're here today because the earlier you start to treat shingles, the better the prognosis and the shorter the illness. It can be excruciatingly painful, as Deb's finding out. So bed rest for you, young lady, a dark room, painkillers and sleep.'

Debbie groaned. 'I can't just stop. How's Cam supposed to run the station *and* look after the tourists?'

Kate reached out and squeezed Debbie's shoulder, hating that she had to break the bad news to the hard-working couple. 'Debbie, you're in quarantine. The tourists can't be in the house while you're infectious. Each blister contains the virus and just like chickenpox you have to stay isolated.'

'But we're fully booked.' Debbie dropped her head into her hands.

Cam sat down next to Deb and wrapped her in a hug, his large arms enveloping the petite woman.

Did Debbie know how lucky she was to be loved like that? Kate pushed away the errant and slightly jealous thought.

Cam stroked Deb's hair. 'I'll call in Beth Johnson and she can cook for the guests in the shearing shed—that will keep everyone out of the house.'

Debbie burst into tears.

Cam looked bewildered as his usually in-control wife sobbed on his shoulder. He patted her back. 'The tourists will be fine, love, honest.'

Debbie sniffed. 'But I'm going to miss Brenda's fundraiser on Saturday, and I can't even visit her. If Brenda got something like this now, with her immune system whacked from chemo, she could die.'

Kate exchanged a worried look with Baden. Debbie was clearly exhausted, sick and overwrought.

'Well, she'd get pretty sick and you're right, you wouldn't want to risk it.' Baden produced some tablets and poured a glass of water. 'Take these, Debbie, they'll ease the pain. We'll leave you with the famciclovir, some cream for the rash if it gets really itchy, and some strong painkillers. I want you to phone the base tomorrow to report in.' Baden suddenly became unusually stern, his gaze fixed on Debbie and Cameron. 'If the rash develops near your eye, you're to radio the base immediately.'

'Why?' Debbie raised her head from Cam's shoulder.

'There is a slight chance you might develop shingles running through your eye and if you did it's serious and we would need to fly you to the Base Hospital to see an ophthalmologist.'

Fright raced across Debbie's face. 'How can I stop that from happening?'

Baden sighed. 'You can't, but you *can* take the antiviral medication and get plenty of sleep, which will help your body heal.'

'I'll make sure she takes the tablets and rests, Baden.' Cam pulled his wife to her feet. 'You go to bed, honey.'

'I'll come and get your room set up, close the blinds and make sure you have what you need.' Kate picked up a jug and a glass and followed Debbie down the hall into a large bedroom. French doors opened out onto the veranda to catch the breeze on hot summer nights.

'You put your nightie on and I'll make your bed.' Kate pulled the bottom sheet taut and executed hospital corners. She always got a great sense of satisfaction from making beds and settling patients so they were comfortable. She pulled the curtains closed, blocking out the light to lessen Debbie's photophobia.

'Oh, that bed looks so good.' Debbie sank into it.

Kate tucked her in. 'The analgesics will kick in soon and they might make you feel dizzy so don't go trying to do anything, OK?'

'Yes, Sister.' Debbie snuggled into the pillows and then fixed Kate with a piercing look. 'That Baden's a bit of a dish, isn't he?'

Kate groaned inwardly. Ever since Debbie had married Cam she'd been trying to matchmake everyone else. Initially Kate had been safe from Deb's scheming because she'd been married, but not any more. 'I suppose he is if you like the rakish dark-haired look.'

Debbie raised her brows. 'And you don't?'

I adore it. 'I think it's dangerous.' She set up the jug of water and put it on the bedside table along with a little hand bell she'd found on the bookshelf.

Debbie adjusted her top sheet. 'Now, that's where you're

wrong. You're mistaking danger for adventure. Don't you think it's time you tried some adventure, Kate?'

'Shane gave me enough adventure to last a lifetime, Deb. I don't want complications, I want a quiet life.' She tucked the sheet in briskly, hoping to put an end to the conversation.

'Shane gave you grief, sweetie, not adventure. There's a big difference.' Debbie squeezed her hand and yawned. 'Just think about it.' Her eyes fluttered closed.

Kate quietly closed the door behind her and rested against it for a moment. *Don't you think it's time you tried some adventure?* For a few moments the idea played across her mind, weaving daydreams and delicious thoughts.

It's ludicrous. She pushed herself off the door. She didn't want to get involved again and even if she did, Baden wasn't offering her anything, let alone adventure. It was just the strong painkillers making Debbie babble on and she shouldn't be taking anything Deb said seriously.

There was no point thinking about adventure with a raven-haired doctor. The *only* thing she should be thinking about was getting home tonight and making some final calls for the drive-in fundraising night. Surely Glen must be arriving soon.

Baden passed Kate her satellite phone, which started ringing the moment she walked back into the kitchen. He watched her take the call. He'd observed her so often over the last few weeks he could now recognise many of her expressions. Rapid blinking meant unexpected news.

She snapped down the antenna of the phone. 'That was Glen. He's worried about the weather so he wants us to meet him at the old strip out by Dog Tired Hut.'

'Dog Tired Hut?' Baden laughed at the name. 'Why would there even be an airstrip at such a place?'

'My great-grandfather built that hut after a particularly dif-

ficult droving season.' Cam rinsed out the teacups. 'He used it
for rest and shelter on the big drive south. These days when we're
mustering, we use the hut as a lunch stop and an Av-gas station.
The helicopter lands there to refuel so the strip's in good nick.'
Cameron glanced out to the west. 'I don't like the look of those
clouds, though. Still, Glen will have seen the radar so he must
reckon he can get in before the rain turns the strip to mush.'

Baden followed Cam's stare. 'Those clouds have come
across the sky every day for a week, just teasing us with the
idea of rain.'

'Yeah, but Dad was complaining of aching knees this
morning and as a rain predictor, they rarely fail.'

'That's pretty scientific, Cam.' Baden raised his brows at his
host.

Cam looked suitably embarrassed. 'I know, but despite my
postgraduate qualifications in agriculture, including a unit on
weather patterns, Dad's knees are the most constant predictor.'
He fished a set of keys out of his pocket. 'Take Betsy out to the
hut and I'll get out there later in the week to collect her.'

He tossed the keys to Kate. 'You'd better drive her but teach
the doc the trick with the column shift so he's set for next time.'

Kate caught the keys and grabbed her gear. 'I'll go and
sweet-talk her into starting first time. Keep a close eye on Deb,
Cam, and ring us any time.' She peered into the sky. 'I hope
you get some rain but not until I'm home.'

He nodded slowly in agreement. 'Take care.'

Baden shook Cam's hand. 'Thanks, mate. See you next month.'

He followed Kate out to Betsy. Cameron's door-less ute was
legendary but this was the first time he'd had ever had to use
it. He put their medical bags in the back tray under an old
hessian wheat sack before sliding in next to Kate on the old
bench seat.

She grinned and handed him a surgical mask.

He turned it over in his hand. 'What's this for?'

'Dust. Move away from the door to avoid the worst and find somewhere to hang on because there are no seat belts.'

Somewhere to hang on. His gaze settled on Kate. He quickly took advantage of a legitimate invitation to sit really close to her. His palm itched to settle on her thigh.

Moving toward her, he slung his arm casually along the back of the seat. Faint vestiges of her floral perfume wafted toward him. How did she manage to smell so good after a day spent in heat and dust? The question lay unanswered as he lost himself in her scent.

Her brow creased in concentration as she pushed the key into the ignition. 'Right, then.' She patted the dashboard. 'Sweetie, you're going to behave for me today, aren't you?'

He pulled his sunglasses down over his eyes, his mouth twitching. 'You're talking to a *car.*'

'Shh, she's really sensitive. She comes through on emergencies, but if she knows it's just a regular drive she can play up.'

He put on his mock serious expression. 'Perhaps I should introduce myself to put her at ease?'

She shot him a derisive look, but humour spun through her eyes. 'That won't be necessary as you're not driving, but it's absolutely essential when you do drive.' Her fine-boned hands closed around the large steering-wheel. 'Now, you pump the accelerator twice before you turn her on.' Kate's foot pumped then she bit her lip and turned the key.

The engine roared into life and Kate gave him a broad smile of delight. He loved they way she got such a thrill out of the little things in life. 'Well done. What's next?'

'Put your mask on.' She pulled her own on and then pushed the column shift toward the wheel and down and Betsy moved forward. 'The problem isn't getting into first gear but into second. Relax the pressure on the gearstick as you pass neutral.'

He watched the concentration crease her forehead as she changed into second. 'You seem to know a lot about cars.'

She laughed. 'I know squat about cars but Emily taught me all about Betsy. She's the one who will whip up the bonnet and fiddle about. I guess it's the legacy of five brothers.' She relaxed as she manoeuvred the shift into third gear, her leg brushing his. 'No, I'm a real girl. If the battery plays up I can hit the terminals with my shoe and that's about it.'

'Does it work?'

She suddenly looked sheepish. 'It usually gets a man to come to my aid who's prepared to get his hands grimy and jump-start the car.'

'Ah! So all this feminist independence is a front.' He loved teasing her.

'No.' Her voice sounded huffy but her eyes sparkled above the mask. 'I am completely independent, except for cars. I just hate getting my hands covered in grease, or anything dirty for that matter.'

'But it just washes off.' He shook his head. 'You sound just like Sasha.'

'Wise girl, your daughter.'

Her high-wattage smile radiating from her eyes hit him soul deep. Her eyes reflected laughter and affection, backlit by something more. Instinctively his hand curled around her shoulder, easing his body into hers, closing the slight gap between them.

As the ute bounced over unmade road and plumes of dust billowed out, conversation became impossible. Kate's body was touching his as she headed Betsy toward the hut. He could feel the rise and fall of her chest, strands of her hair blown by the wind caressed his cheek and her soft skin lay against his own.

All thoughts of his work responsibilities and his worries about Sasha drained out of him. Nothing existed except the two of them alone on this long, straight and dusty track. *Just the two of them.*

It felt…right

He hoped it would take a really long time to get to Dog Tired Hut.

The rain started to fall three kilometres from their destination. Kate sat forward, concentrating on the track that was fast becoming red, sucking mud.

For the last twenty minutes she'd driven with Baden's arm curved around her and his leg pressing against hers, just as if they were two teenagers sneaking off together. She hated it that it felt so good. So right.

'I don't like the look of this rain.' She scanned the horizon, hoping to see the plane. 'I thought Glen would have been waiting for us.' A niggle of anxiety skated through her.

'He can't be too far away.' Baden gave her shoulder a reassuring squeeze.

Occasional drops that splattered them turned into driving rain that came straight into the ute as they approached the hut. Kate pulled to a stop, the wheels skidding in the mud. She whipped off her mask. 'Let's make a run for the hut. We'll be drier in there.'

Her feet hit the ground and she immediately sank into ankle-deep mud. 'Oh, yuck.' She looked sadly at the red mud that had trapped her shoes. Pulling each foot out with an audible slurp, she gingerly made her way to the back of the ute.

Baden picked up her medical bag and passed it to her. She extended her hand to grab the handle but her grip was slick with rain and it slipped. She leaned forward, reaching to catch the bag before it sank into the mud, but she overbalanced. Her feet gave way and she fell head first into the quagmire.

'Are you OK?' Baden extended his hand, his lips compressed, trying to suppress the laughter that shook his body.

She glanced down at herself to see red clay caking her from shoulder to toe. Rain and mud plastered her uniform to her, making her look like a cross between a mud wrestler and a wet T-shirt competitor. Her fingers pulled uselessly at her clinging shirt, which hid little. 'I can't believe I did this. I'm filthy.'

Baden's hand gripped her wrist and he pulled her to her feet, his face alive with amusement and a flash of appreciation. 'At least your hands aren't covered in grease.'

His laughter carried away her dismay and she joined in. 'I think I can add mud to my list of icky substances I don't like being covered in.' Rain ran down her neck, as well as into her shoes. She tossed her head back and spread her arms out wide, willing the plane to arrive, attempting to wash herself at the same time.

'Come on, you're soaked. Let's go inside.' Holding his medical kit with one hand and her hand with the other, he jogged toward the hut and unbolted the door.

The satellite phone rang in her pocket as they stepped over the threshold. Swallowing her horror, she wiped her muddy hands on the one bit of her shorts that was dry and punched the answer button. 'Glen, I'm on speakerphone. We're at the hut but where are you?'

'Sorry, Kate, Baden, I've had to divert due to the weather. It's very local but I can't risk the plane on the strip. I can pick you up from McCurdy's.'

Baden frowned. 'But that's one hundred kilometres from here and the track will be a bog.'

Kate nodded and spoke to Glen. 'Even if we could get there, which we doubt we can, we couldn't make it before nightfall.'

'I can't land at night unless it's an emergency. Sorry, guys, but I think you're stuck for the night.' Glen's apologetic voice came down the line. 'We'll reassess everything in the morning.'

She glanced at Baden and they spoke at the same moment. 'Sasha.'

'Glen, we have limited battery life. Sasha Tremont needs to be collected from after-school care and looked after for the night. Can you organise that?'

'Sure. I'll radio Jen, who'll sort it out. Don't worry, Baden, she'll be fine, and my kids will love having a visitor for the night. Meanwhile, enjoy your outback adventure, guys. Over and out.'

The line went dead.

Baden started to pace and his hand tugged at his hair. 'Hell. How can I be a doctor and a decent father? She hasn't ever slept over at Glen and Jen's and she shouldn't even have to.'

Kate put her hand on his arm as an overwhelming need to reassure him settled in her belly. 'It's OK. These things happen in the outback. If you were a plumber you could have got stranded by this rain and washed-out roads. Sasha knows the Jacobses. Hannah's in her class and they're in the same patrol at Guides. She'll love having an unexpected sleepover.'

He sighed, his expression not quite in agreement. 'I suppose so but I promised her we'd make toffee tonight for the stall. I hate letting her down.'

A flash of irritation sparked in her. Why was he this hard on himself? 'You're not letting her down. You're raising a kid who knows she's loved and who goes with the flow. At Guides, she's the one who copes with unexpected things when the others panic or just get frustrated because something hasn't gone according to plan. She knows you're not in any danger so she won't be stressing. In fact, if I know Sasha, she'll be organising Jen and the kids to make the toffee.'

A wry smile tugged at his lips as his apprehensive expression slowly faded. 'She organises me all the time so you're probably right. She'll be making the most out of this unexpected situation.'

Tension seemed to flow out of his body and an unfamiliar aura of lightness surrounded him. His eyes danced, his brow cleared and a sinful smile clung to his lips.

The change was intoxicating. She'd never seen him look like this. It was as if he'd discarded the burdens that had been clinging to him from the moment she'd met him.

He glanced around at the spartan hut. 'Meanwhile, *we* need to make the most of this situation.'

The double entendre of his words hung in the air. Her heart hammered hard against her chest.

His desire-fuelled gaze came back to rest on her. She could feel his eyes travelling the length of her body. Her skin, cool from the rain and mud, heated up so fast she could swear she could hear the water sizzle.

He stepped in close. 'I think the first thing we need to do is get out of these wet clothes.' His words rolled out, low and husky.

She swallowed hard at his crystal-clear intent. 'Really? We don't have spare clothes.'

He tucked her wet hair behind her ear. 'It would be the responsible thing to do. After all, we don't want to get hypothermia.'

Every nerve ending was firing off rounds of heat and the idea of hypothermia seemed ridiculous, but her body started to shiver. She couldn't tell if it was from cold or anticipation.

He tilted his head toward the old bed, covered with a couple of even older rag quilts. His grin—one of sheer devilment and daring—raced across his face. 'I think that for *tonight* this is our best option.'

She stared up at him, sinking into eyes so blue, completely

caught in their hypnotic effect. *You're weak, Kate. This is just a moment in time. He's only offering one night.*

But he could have asked her almost anything at that point and she would have said yes. She was done with being sensible. Being sensible had only brought her heartache. She didn't want marriage and commitment and neither did he. No promises were being made, just an agreement of a stolen moment in time.

I need this. I'm taking this one moment in time because it will never come my way again. The memory will keep me warm in the lonely nights ahead.

'So you think that snuggling up in that bed for this *one night* would be the best idea?'

His expression registered the deal on the table. 'I do. Body heat is powerful stuff, Kate.' His finger drew a feather-soft trail down her cheek.

She swayed toward him, placing her hands on his chest, her fingers feeling the solid muscle beneath his wet shirt. 'But I'm all muddy.'

'I'll wash you.'

Blood roared in her ears at the image his words created. Then his mouth came down onto hers, his tongue caressing her lips with soft and delicate touches, making her feel cherished and adored. Sending waves of longing pounding through her, setting her legs trembling.

Her hands found his hair, his curls all wet and soft under her fingers. She opened her mouth to his, welcoming him, giving herself to him, letting him take away a year of pain and loneliness. Taking a moment in time for herself.

Her hand found the buttons on his shirt and she started to undo each one, her fingers stiff and shaking with a mixture of cold and need.

Still his mouth stayed on hers, creating sensations she'd

never known. Aching pleasure built inside her and her body quivered, longing for him to touch more than just her lips.

As if reading her mind, Baden eased his lips from hers and trailed kisses along her jaw. He murmured against her neck, 'You're beautiful. You're beautiful covered in mud, you'd be beautiful covered in grease, and you've been driving me crazy for the last three and a half months.'

'Have I?' She needed to hear him say it again, to drive away the nightmare of her marriage.

His hands slid under her shirt, dextrously releasing the catch on her bra. 'You have and I can't wait to see all of you, muddy or not.'

A thrill zipped through her, heading straight to her core. She pushed his shirt from his shoulders and pressed her lips to his chest, tasting rain mixed with salt and feeling taut muscle under skin. Hers for tonight.

He pulled her shirt over her head, dropping it onto a chair before pulling her close, his hands splayed against her back, kneading her spine.

Skin against skin. Breast against chest.

Waves of need crashed through her.

She fought to memorise every moment of this brief time with him but as pleasure surged through her, she let herself be swept away on a tide of bliss.

'You're cold.' He pulled her toward the bed and with a scrambling of hands—belts, bra, shorts and pants cascaded into a heap. Laughing, they both fell onto the bed, the old springs creaking under their weight and the mattress sinking in the middle, rolling them together.

Legs entwined. Cold flesh met cold flesh, instantly flaring into heat.

'Let me warm you,' he murmured gently into her hair as his

hand cupped her breast. His thumb brushed her nipple, which instantly rose to his touch.

White lights danced in front of her eyes as rivers of wonder flowed through her. Wonder that he touched her with such tenderness, wonder that he wanted her.

She wanted him. Her body vibrated with need as her hands raced all over him, touching him, feeling him, making sure this was all real but knowing it was really an illusion—a fantasy in a moment of time.

She didn't care.

He caught her hands loosely and held them above her head, his focus entirely on her pleasure. With a low guttural moan he trailed kisses across each breast and then closed his mouth softly over her tingling nipple, his tongue gently lashing the sensitive nub.

A groan of ecstasy escaped her parted lips, the sound completely foreign to her. Nothing she had ever experienced before had been like this.

She gripped his shoulders as she unconsciously rose toward him, never wanting him to stop.

He raised his head, his eyes simmering with wickedness. 'So that works for you, does it? What about this?' He dipped his head, his tongue trailing a curving path past her belly button and beyond.

Her hands frantically gripped his head as he wove his magic. It was too fast, she wanted to savour it moment by moment but her body disagreed. Her mind shut down completely, driving out all thoughts, all arguments, all common sense. Her mind gave over to her body to glory in everything being offered. She took it all greedily, like a thirsty person took water, not knowing when it might be offered again.

Layer upon layer of tingling, glorious sensation built on

itself deep inside her, like a furnace being constantly stoked, intensifying with every stroke of his tongue, taking her higher and higher until she teetered on a precipice, sheer pleasure and pain blurring. She called his name, then shattered into a million shards of light as ribbons of liquid paradise poured through her, mellowing her completely.

She lay back on the lumpy pillow, Baden's smiling face above her, looking very self-satisfied. The wondrous feelings suddenly faded, leaving her muscles twitching, aching and empty. She reached for him. 'That was very nice, thank you, but I think you can do better.'

He brushed her damp hair from her face. 'Is that so?'

'Hmm, yes.' She traced the contours of his face, the pads of her fingers absorbing him like a blind person absorbed Braille.

He lowered his head and whispered deliciously wicked suggestions into her ear.

All thoughts of teasing faded as her body thrummed with aching need for him. She rose up against him, welcoming him into her, needing him to complete her in an age-old way. Glorying in his need of her.

Together they created a rhythm that drove them higher and higher until they cried out together and tumbled over the edge, freefalling—forever entwined.

Baden stoked the fire and spread Kate's rinsed clothes out along the fireguard to dry. Kate stood beside the fire wrapped in a quilt, all rosy pink after her wash in the hipbath, all dark hair and dark eyes. She looked lush and delectable.

Memories of how lush and delectable she was had him pulling her into his arms. He sat down with her cuddled on his lap.

'Your clothes will be dry soon.'

She snuggled against him. 'Thanks for looking after me. The

bath was divine and somehow you even made instant noodles taste palatable.'

He laughed and dropped a kiss into her hair, which smelt of lavender shampoo. 'I think you were just so hungry you weren't as discerning as usual.'

'Perhaps.' She stifled a yawn. 'What time is it?'

He glanced at his watch. 'Nine o'clock. Why?'

She put a finger to his lips before slipping off his lap and pulling him to his feet. 'Come and look at this.' With the quilt trailing behind her like a bride's train, she padded over to the door and stepped outside.

He'd never seen a sky like it. Silver lights danced across the ink-black sky. Twinkling stars in all their sparkling glory rained their light down on them. The Southern Cross constellation hovered on the horizon and the moon was yet to rise. 'It's beautiful.'

Kate picked up his hand and pointed with it. 'Look over there.'

He peered up, his eyes straining to discern something special amongst the mass of stars. Then he saw a streak moving across the sky. He couldn't believe his eyes. 'Is that a comet?'

She turned to him, her face alive with excitement. 'Yes, and not only is tonight the best night to see it, we're out here with no light pollution.'

He pulled her close, loving the way her curves fitted into him. 'It's a special night all round.'

She laid her head on his shoulder. 'One worth remembering.'

Her quiet words unexpectedly speared him. *One night.* It was what they both wanted, what they had both agreed to. Neither of them was able to offer more. He couldn't risk loving again, he had to protect Sasha. Kids loved easily, but as Kate didn't want a relationship he couldn't risk Sasha getting attached. Another loss could devastate her.

But he had tonight. They had less than twelve hours before real life returned. Before he was a doctor again, before he was a father again. Before life returned to what it had been.

So why the hell was he out here, looking at stars?

He swung her into his arms and took her back inside.

CHAPTER NINE

'MINE!' Sasha dived for the ball, catching it and hugging it to her chest with one arm as she swam with the other toward the water polo goal.

'Not likely.' Baden ducked under the water and came up next to her, tickling her around the waist until she surrendered the ball.

'That's cheating.' Her indignation came out on a wave of laughter as she grabbed her father by the feet.

Baden disappeared under the water in a haze of bubbles, the ball bouncing up to the surface of the water.

Kate grabbed it, shimmied up onto the edge of the pool and sat watching father and daughter do battle, not even aware their target had been poached. She hated to admit it but she could watch them together for hours. Baden was a wonderful father and he and Sasha had a very close relationship, which wasn't surprising, considering what they'd both been through.

It couldn't be easy, raising a daughter on your own, and she was happy to help but Baden kept Sasha to himself. Stupidly, she couldn't shake the irrational thought that after their wonderful night together at Dog Tired Hut, he might just want to spend a bit more time with her. That he might want Sasha to spend some more time with her. She sighed. It seemed that was just a giant flight of her imagination.

The only reason Sasha and Baden were swimming in her pool was because they'd spent the morning making sausage rolls in her kitchen for the drive-in night. And the only reason that Baden had come was because of the purpose of the night. He was committed to the ovarian cancer fundraiser. He didn't want anyone to lose a loved one like he had.

Lose a wife.

Baden might have *made* love to her three nights ago but he was still *in* love with his wife. So much so that he was still trying to live his life as if she were still alive.

She didn't think it was healthy for him or Sasha but, then again, what did she know? Her marriage had been a disaster and his, she suspected, had been wonderful, so it was like comparing apples to oranges. She couldn't imagine what it would be like to lose someone who completed you.

Baden completes you.

The random thought thundered through her. Immediately, every part of her tried to eject it from her brain. No, it wasn't possible—she wouldn't allow that kind of thinking.

Sasha and Baden both surfaced from their underwater chase, spluttering and still trying to dunk each other when they saw Kate holding the ball.

They pulled themselves out of the pool and sat next to her, flanking her, catching their breath. Cosy warmth spread through her as Sasha's arm wrapped around her waist and she cuddled in close.

'Lost something?' Kate smirked as she stroked the ball, the thrill of oneupmanship streaking through her. 'You two are hopeless. You're so busy trying to outdo each other that you took your eye off the main game.'

Sasha giggled. 'You sound like a mum, Kate. My mum used to say Dad and I were too competitive.'

Kate surreptitiously glanced at Baden, expecting the usual tension to enter him like it always did whenever Annie was mentioned. But his demeanour didn't change at all.

He gave a deep, rumbling laugh. 'I can still beat you, Sash.'

'Wanna bet?' Sasha flicked water at him with her feet.

Kate spun the ball on her index finger, taunting them both. 'I'm thinking that as neither of you actually *have* the ball then I win.'

Baden and Sasha instantly exchanged knowing looks and suddenly their arms circled Kate. For a moment she was cocooned and a flash of what it might be like to be part of their lives spooled through her mind. Loved by a man who was defined by his caring. Mother to a girl with great spirit and determination. Part of a loving team—part of a family.

Then the arms tightened around her and she felt herself moving. 'Hey!' But her cry was lost as she was pushed into the water by four hands and then tickled mercilessly. She kicked to the surface. 'You two fight dirty.'

'Yeah.' Baden grinned and pulled her close, his arms and legs immobilising her against him. 'Sash, I've got her, you get the ball.'

Sasha ducked under and tickled Kate under the arms.

Kate released the ball in self-protection as her chest muscles ached with laughter. 'Not fair—two against one.'

'Got it, Dad.' Sasha swam toward the goal.

Kate expected Baden to swim after Sasha, but he unexpectedly stayed put.

She looked up into eyes full of fun that suddenly darkened with longing. His arms pinned her against his length, nothing between them but thin Lycra.

Her blood pounded in her ears as it raced his heat through her, waking every part of her. Reminding her of the night they'd spent together and refuelling the need that simmered permanently under the surface into boiling yearning.

Water dripped from his flattened curls onto her face, the droplets making a slow and erotic trail down her cheek. With each breath his chest rose and fell against hers, his heart beating hard, matching her own.

For the shortest moment he looked over her head toward Sasha, who was concentrating hard on shooting a goal, then his gaze returned, searing her with need. He swooped his lips down against hers, hot, hard and urgent. He kissed her, seizing her breath, branding her with his touch and taste and tantalising her with a glimpse of what she knew he could offer.

Then he spun her out of his arms and swam like a man possessed toward Sasha. 'Great goal, sweetie.' He gave her a high five. 'What a team.'

Panting for breath and completely stunned, Kate trod water as the world regained its axis, and all vivid colours faded. Ordinary life returned, looking pale and wan.

His naked need stayed with her. She recognised that need, she was intimate with it as it mirrored her own. She knew in the depth of her soul he wanted her in his arms. That one night had not been enough.

And she so wanted to be back in his arms, feeling cherished and treasured. Back in the arms of this wonderful man who'd quietly supported her as she'd faced the town. He'd pushed her to take a risk, but he'd been with her every step of the way. This brilliant, caring doctor, this considerate and adventurous lover, and this devoted father with a huge capacity to love.

She loved him.

She gripped the side of the pool as the muscles in her legs went weak with realisation and stopped treading water.

Oh, this wasn't good. She rested her head on the curve of the bull-nose pavers. She'd fallen in love with a man locked in the past. A man whose love for his dead wife still coloured his decisions and governed how he raised his daughter. A man who kept himself and his daughter locked away from the love she had to offer.

For weeks she'd tried not to love him. He didn't want to be loved and she knew only too well that love didn't work for her. But despite everything she'd tried, love had sneaked in. She loved him and she loved his daughter.

Sasha.

Sasha is my top priority now. Baden's determined voice resonated in her head. Sasha came first, which was how it should be. But what if she could show him that Sasha came first with her as well? Could that possibly open his eyes to the idea that he could love again? That he could love her? The thought embedded in her mind, sinking down deep with penetrating roots.

'You're cutting it really fine.' Gwen Lloyd, the sister in charge of the Opal Ridge Bush Nursing Hospital, filled the burette on Hughie's IV, diluting the penicillin infusion.

Baden checked his watch. 'I'll just make it as I've only got Dimity to assess and I can dictate the referrals at home.'

'Sorry, me sugars have gone haywire, Doc. It's this bloody cough.' The old miner sat forward as his frail frame shuddered with a racking cough.

Today's clinic had been frantic. The current virus had swept the small town and everyone had called into the clinic, hoping he could prescribe a magic cure. For most people all he could prescribe was TLC, bed rest and plenty of fluids. But the elderly had been hit harder and he had two suspected cases of pneumonia.

'Cough that goop up, Hughie.' Gwen put her hand on Hughie's bony back and held a specimen jar under his mouth.

Baden had started Hughie on penicillin but he needed to drop the specimen of sputum off at Warragurra Base Pathology for an accurate culture. He put the small plastic container with its bright yellow lid into a cooler bag. 'I'll ring through the results. We might need to change the antibiotics.'

Gwen nodded. 'I'll call you if he doesn't improve.'

Baden put his hand over Hughie's work-scarred one. 'Don't you worry about me, Hughie. I've got enough time to get back to Warragurra. You only need to concentrate on getting well.'

The old man slumped back onto the pillows, his eyes bright with fever. 'Don't you think it's time you got yourself another wife, lad, instead of all this rushing about? She could be looking after your little girl.'

Baden forced a smile to his face. All his elderly patients who lived alone thought he should have a wife. 'It's a different world, Hughie. Even if I did marry, which I'm not going to do, my wife would probably be working and I'd still have to collect Sasha.'

'Humph.' Hughie wasn't impressed. 'Well, all this gadding about, it's not what a family is all about.' He closed his eyes, ending the conversation.

Baden sighed. 'Gwen will look after you, Hughie, and hopefully we won't have to fly you to Warragurra. Remember to eat all the food so your blood sugar is stable.'

Thirty minutes later, he kept his eye on the speedometer as he sped down the bitumen road toward Warragurra. A speeding ticket was the last thing he needed on top of his frantic day. He wished he could drive and dictate at the same time. All the paperwork would have him up until midnight.

Paperwork Kate usually did for him if she was rostered on with him. But Kate never came with him to Opal Ridge. Today she'd stayed in Warragurra, running an in-service for the nurses. Gwen did a great job but she wasn't Kate.

Kate.

Kate, who four nights ago had made love to him with a passion that had taken his breath away. Together, their lust for each other should have set the old hut on fire. Yet, when he thought about their stolen time, those few hours in the outback, it was the joy of holding her close, the wonder of her comforting heat snuggled against him and the banter and serious discussions late into the night that stayed uppermost in his mind.

But it had been a 'once only' night—they'd both been adamant about that. So why did his arms ache at not being able to hold her?

Today had seemed twice as long without her. He'd missed her friendly smile and her jokes and their conversation. They talked about all sorts of things and today he'd wanted to get her advice on the best way to broach the topic of periods with Sasha. Last night he'd tried, but Sasha had immediately changed the subject. He could just see her saying, 'Ee-uuww,' Dad,' and escaping to her room when he tried again. Kate taught puberty education and probably had some natty pink sample pack he could give Sasha, as well as a few tips.

Sasha talked about her all the time and since Kate had taught her how to French braid her hair, she proudly wore it that way. Kate genuinely seemed to enjoy Sasha's company.

He turned into School Road and slowed to the obligatory forty-kilometre school zone speed limit. Sasha, who was playing outside, gave him a wave and ran back inside to get her bag. Baden followed and signed the in-out book.

'Thanks, Gloria, see you next week.' Baden handed over an envelope with the week's fees enclosed to the after-school care co-ordinator.

Gloria spoke, sotto voce. 'I thought without Erin we were going to have problems, but Sasha's the happiest and most settled she's ever been.'

Baden nodded. 'I think that Guides and swimming has helped.'

'Hmm.' The experienced teacher vacillated. 'I think there's more to it than that.'

Sasha reappeared from the bag cage. 'Thanks, Mrs Davidson.' She pulled on her backpack. 'Are you coming to the drive-in on Saturday night?'

The matronly woman smiled. 'I wouldn't miss it for anything, dear.' She suddenly had a far-away look in her eyes. 'I remember going to the drive-in with my Stan and a big box of chocolates.'

'Oh, we have heaps of great food, Mrs D. Kate, my Guide leader, well, actually she's dad's nurse but really she's my friend, she has had us cooking loads of yummy stuff.'

Baden smiled at how kids needed to mention every connection they had to people. He would have just said 'Kate.'

'That's wonderful, dear.' She shot Baden a meaningful look.

He had no idea what it meant. Sasha was very excited about the fundraiser but so was the whole town. Kate had organised the Guides into a food-creating machine. He put his hand on his daughter's shoulder. 'Honey, we have to go.'

They waved goodbye and headed to the car. As Baden turned back onto the road he remembered the sputum container. 'We just have to go to the hospital to drop something off.'

'OK. Will Kate be there?' Sasha selected a CD from the collection.

'I don't know. I didn't see her today.' He flicked down the sun visor against the glaring late afternoon sun.

She slid in the CD. 'You like Kate, don't you, Dad?'

He slowed down at a give-way sign and checked for oncoming traffic, his mind half on the conversation. 'Of course I do. She's a good friend to both of us.'

'She must get lonely in that big house.'

He waited for the oncoming car to pass and then turned right into Settlement Street. 'She's got Rupert and Snowy.'

'Yeah, but they don't talk.'

He squinted through the sun glare, thinking he really should wash the windscreen from the inside. 'Well, she's thinking of selling Sandon anyway.'

Sasha spun so fast that her seat belt snapped tight. 'No, she can't do that!' Her voice sounded horrified. 'She invited Erin and me for a sleepover after the fundraiser and I've already chosen a room.' Her voice started to rise. 'And she said I could visit whenever I want to and ride Thumper and…'

He sighed at her reaction. If only Mrs Davidson could see Sasha now. 'Calm down, sweetheart. I just said she might sell Sandon. It's her home and her life and her decision. It's nothing to do with us.'

'But it's such a cool house and she should stay. I love it there.'

An irrational irritation zinged through him. He and Sasha lived in a lovely house full of love. 'There are more important things in life than a nice house, a swimming pool and horses. Besides, when we visit Kate we're just guests at Sandon. It's not like we're part of her family.'

Sasha folded her arms across her chest. 'I *know* that, Dad. But I still think that Kate is lonely. She needs someone.'

Am image of Kate in the arms of another man speared him so sharply he flinched but then her words on marriage pounded him. She had no plans for another relationship. 'I think she's happy with her life the way it is, Sasha.'

'I don't know, Dad.' Sasha sounded unconvinced. 'I think she needs someone.' Her green eyes flashed with conviction. 'Just like you need someone.'

His throat dried at the unsubtle matchmaking. Sasha was twelve, with no idea what relationships meant or how they would affect her. How another person in their life would take his focus away from her. 'I don't need anyone, honey. You and I are a team and I'm happy just the way things are.'

But the words sounded unexpectedly hollow to his ears.

Warragurra had been buzzing for days. Finally the drive-in night arrived and kids and adults alike bounced with excitement.

A huge semi-trailer with an enormous screen hanging from one side was parked in the paddock next to the school. The school grounds had been turned into a carnival with white-topped marquees selling everything from sausages in bread to de luxe hamburgers, fizzy drinks to fairy floss and the always popular lolly stall.

Music blared from the loudspeakers and kids charged around the grounds, waving their glow-in-the dark sticks. The pre-movie picnic was in full swing. Nothing this big had happened in Warragurra for a long time. The airport even had a parking problem as so many light planes from outlying stations had flown in for the event. People stood around in groups, enthusiastically chatting, the gathering having a second purpose—breaking the isolation of outback life on the land. Even Shane's parents had come along.

Last week they'd written to Kate, wishing her well for a successful night and enclosing a large cheque as a donation. They might never be close friends but at least the rift seemed to have eased.

The Guides were helping out at a variety of stalls with their parents' assistance. Kate had left it up to Sasha which stall she wanted to work on with Baden, but Sasha had been adamant she was working with Kate. Baden hadn't said a word. He'd arrived with Sasha two hours ago, donned a barbecue apron that made him look like he was wearing a dinner suit and took his place at the hotplate with Phoebe Walton's father, Richard. He looked as mouth-watering as the food he was cooking.

Whenever she turned his way he gave her a grin and a flourish with the tongs. Kate dragged her gaze away from him for the zillionth time. What she really wanted to do was throw her arms around his neck and trail kisses along his jaw, his neck, his chest... She pulled her attention back to assembling souvlaki, Malaysian satay and hamburgers with all the trimmings, including pineapple and beetroot.

Sasha stood next to her, beaming at the customers as she happily took their money. 'Enjoy your dinner and remember to stock up at the lolly stall before the movie.'

Kate gave her a quick hug. 'You're a born salesperson, Sasha.'

The girl seemed to stand a bit taller. 'This is just so totally awesome. I've never had so much fun.'

Kate's heart swelled. 'I've had a lot of fun working with you and getting to know you. It's great that we've made friends and we're helping to raise money for a really worthwhile cause.'

Her elfin face became serious for a moment. 'I know Mum would be really pleased I've done this. She always said that helping others made you feel good about yourself.'

The more Kate learned about Annie Tremont the more she thought she would have liked her had she known her. 'Your mum sounds like a clever woman.'

'She was, but so are you, Kate. I couldn't have done anything like this without your help. You're not really moving, are you?'

The question surprised her. 'I wasn't planning on moving. Why?'

Sasha looked a bit embarrassed. 'Oh, it was just something Dad said.'

The memory of the time she'd told Baden about Shane came

flooding back. 'I once said to your dad that I was thinking I might move but I don't feel that way any more.'

Sasha unexpectedly flung her arms around her waist. 'I'm *so* glad you're not going. I'd really miss you if you left.'

The intensity of the heartfelt words stunned her and she treasured them, holding them close to her heart.

'Kate, Sasha, we're starving here.' Des Cincotta stood at the front of the queue, a teal green turban on his head and a smile a mile wide as he held tightly to Brenda's hand. Behind them stood a long line of people, all wearing the same teal green turbans.

'Oh, those head scarfs are so funky.' Sasha gazed at them with longing.

Brenda pulled two turbans out of her bag. 'I have one for both of you. The big one is for Kate and the smaller one is for you, Sasha. I thought it might be a good symbol for remembering your mum and looking to the future.'

The young girl's eyes widened in delight. 'Thanks heaps, Mrs Cincotta.' She immediately turned to Kate. 'Can you help me put it on?'

'Sure.' Kate took off her gloves and wound the material around her own head and then placed the smaller one on Sasha's chestnut hair. 'You look gorgeous.'

'You're just saying that.' Sasha glanced down at her feet.

'No, Kate's absolutely right. You do look gorgeous.'

Baden had wandered over from the barbecue to see what was happening. Fatherly love glowed in his sky-blue eyes.

The familiar lump in her throat formed when Kate caught sight of that look. Father and daughter, a strong bond.

Then his gaze met hers over the top of Sasha's head. 'In fact you both look gorgeous.' Fatherly love suddenly vanished, replaced by a simmering of something stronger. Something she knew was for herself alone.

Her body tingled from the tip of her head down to her toes and then settled deep inside her.

'Don't listen to him, Kate. He's clueless,' Sasha's no-nonsense voice chimed in. 'I can be covered in paint after art and he tells me I'm gorgeous. And no offence but you have sauce on your nose.'

Kate laughed as she wiped away the sauce. But Sasha's comment suddenly brought back Baden's words in a powerful surge. *You'd be beautiful covered in grease.*

Her head spun. If he told his daughter she was gorgeous no matter what, completely unconditionally—did this mean something more? Did he love her? Her heart tripped over itself in happiness at the thought there might be a chance for the three of them as a family.

'So, how many hamburgers, Mr Cincotta?' Sasha focussed back on the important things.

'I reckon twenty-five should do it.' Des handed over a large green note.

Sasha looked stunned as she held the hundred-dollar bill. She carefully put it in the cashbox. 'Hey, Dad, stop slacking, we've got a huge order of twenty-five hamburgers. Come on, Kate, you need to set out the buns.'

'I think we've just been organised.' Baden winked at Kate, and saluted his daughter. 'Coming right up, Miss Tremont.'

Baden walked toward the drinks area, having been released from his cooking duties by Kate as long as he brought back coffee. Although he wasn't sure that a double mocha frappuccino with extra cream really counted as coffee, but he wasn't going to argue with a woman who'd been working flat out since five a.m.

She needed a break; she'd been like a whirling dervish all day.

'Hey, Baden, how's it going?' A woman grabbed his arm, breaking his reverie.

'Emily.' He hugged his ex–flight nurse, taking in her teal turban and a few strands of purple hair that had escaped. 'Great to see you.'

'I hear that Kate Lawson is a star and you're not missing me at all.' She raised her brows, her double meaning clear.

The comment caught him unawares and he found himself clearing his throat. 'If I had to lose you, Kate is a worthy replacement.'

Emily rocked back and laughed. 'Well, that's one way of looking at it. Although you never looked at me the way you look at her.'

His serious doctor voice took over. 'Kate is a valued colleague, just like you are. You're letting your imagination run away with you.'

Emily's smiling face suddenly turned serious. 'No, I don't think I am. I had a *long* wait for my dinner tonight and I watched you at the barbecue. You spent more time looking at Kate than my charred hamburger.'

Hell, had it been that noticeable? He knew he'd lost the battle not to watch her a long time ago, but had he lost the ability to be surreptitious? He tried to deflect Emily with humour. 'Charred! Richard must have cooked that one.'

She put her hand on his arm, her touch and her voice full of understanding. 'I think it's wonderful. You've been alone long enough.'

He breathed in deeply. 'I'm *not* alone. I've got Sasha.'

Emily put her hands on her hips. 'You're being deliberately obtuse. You know what I mean. Your wife died and you miss her, but you've grieved, you've started a new life and it's normal and healthy to want to love again.'

He waited for the usual anger to fizz inside him when people tried to match him up but for some reason it didn't come. That in itself worried him. He changed the subject to something safer. 'So, how's your eldest brother? Did he manage to get the loan for the new dam?'

But Emily wasn't listening to him. She'd turned her head away, her attention one hundred per cent on Linton, who stood on the stage speaking into a microphone. His voice boomed over the PA system. 'Can everyone make their way over to the drive-in area, please? The film's going to start in fifteen minutes.'

Baden raised his brows knowingly. 'So how's Linton?'

Emily turned back with an overly casual shrug. 'No idea. I haven't seen him since he finished his rotation with the Flying Doctors three months ago.'

He crossed his arms and grinned at her. 'Really? I thought I detected more than a casual interest.'

'I think you're letting your imagination run away with you.' She tilted her jaw in the stubborn way he remembered so well and played him at his own game of changing the subject, which spoke volumes. 'Say hi to Sasha for me and I'll catch up with you later.' With a quick wave she walked over to another group of people and made her way to the drive-in paddock.

He joined the coffee queue behind Evelyn Walton. 'Getting a caffeine shot to keep you alert while you supervise the Guides at the movie?'

Evelyn nodded. 'They'll be fine. Richard's filled the back of the ute with foam blocks and cushions and I have enough lollies to keep the dentist in business for the next year.'

Baden ordered the coffees. 'Sounds like we'll be coping with sugar highs.'

Evelyn laughed. 'Probably, but that's all part of the fun.' She moved to the side to wait for her coffee. 'Baden, can you do me a favour?'

'Sure.'

'Richard and I are on duty, along with Sandra, and Hannah's parents, plus there are bound to be other Guide parents who sit with us. Kate's done a huge job getting tonight off the ground and she deserves to watch the movie in a civilised way, rather than being pelted by Guides with foam blocks during the quiet bits.'

He put his hands in his pockets. 'Good luck convincing her not to sit with the Guides.'

Evelyn wrinkled her nose. 'Actually, that's the favour. I want you to convince her.'

A slight tremor of unease ran through him. 'You know Kate, she'll just do what she planned on doing.'

Evelyn picked up her coffee and fixed him with a steely look. 'You're the doctor—tell her she'll collapse from exhaustion or something. Better yet, buy her ice cream and chocolates and nail her to the picnic rug way off to the side so no one can see her to bother her. I'm sure you'll think of something.'

An image of Kate slammed into him. Kate lying down on a picnic rug beside him, her body snuggled against his, her head nestled into his shoulder, her hair tickling his cheek and her lips warm against his own. His breath rushed out of his lungs.

He'd just lost his 'safety in numbers' buffer, the buffer he'd been depending on all day. It had become an increasing battle to keep her out of his arms.

A germ of an idea slowly turned in his brain and the floundering tatters of his resolve to stay away from Kate vanished. He now had the perfect solution that would suit both Kate and him and protect Sasha's feelings.

'Sure, no problem, Evelyn.' He hoped she hadn't noticed just how husky his voice had become.

CHAPTER TEN

KATE'S knees knocked together so hard she was sure people at the back could hear them. She could deal with bleeding bodies and hysterical relatives, she could pull together a huge fund-raising night like tonight, but she dreaded public speaking.

Baden leaned in close and whispered in her ear. 'Just imagine them all naked.'

An image of Baden's golden body illuminated by moonlight came into her mind. Her knocking knees melted on the spot. She threw her hands out wide. 'How is *that* supposed to help?' Her voice started to rise. 'I could never understand how that is a useful tip.'

His eyes sparkled at her, and a grin raced across his cheeks. 'Trust me, just try it.' He gave her a gentle push onto the stage.

She took in a deep breath, tossed her head and walked across the stage, which was really the flatbed of the semi-trailer. Her hand curved tightly around the microphone. 'Ladies and gentlemen. I'm Kate Lawson and…' She looked out onto a sea of over three hundred faces, many of them wearing teal green turbans. Her mind instantly blanked. With a hammering heart she turned her head to the left catching Baden's gaze.

He mouthed at her, 'Think naked,' and gave her a thumbs-up.

She stared straight ahead picturing the crowd only wearing

turbans. She felt a giggle start to rise out of her as her constricted throat relaxed. 'I just want to take a few moments of your time to thank everyone who has been involved in making tonight happen. It wouldn't have been possible without an exceptional team effort and I'm really excited to announce that together you have raised a staggering seven thousand dollars toward finding an early diagnostic test for ovarian cancer.'

Whoops, wolf whistles and car horns sounded as everyone clapped. Somewhere in the crowd a 'Go, Kate' chant started.

Kate waved and the crowd quietened. 'Clinical trials for the test are under way and this money will be used to support these trials, bringing us ever closer to an accurate and fast way to detect this silent disease.' She tucked her hair behind her ear against the early evening breeze. 'But now it's time for the two movies so sit back and enjoy. Thank you very much.'

She almost skipped off the stage toward Baden, so delighted was she to have the speech finished. 'Thank heavens that's over. Now, where are the Guides parked?'

Baden linked his arm through hers and captured her hand. 'The Guides are under the strict supervision of the Waltons and you are off duty.'

'No?' She stared at him and his black brows rose in confirmation. A puff of longing rose up from deep inside her and swirled through her, at odds with a strange sensation of disappointment. She had thought that perhaps she would watch the family-rated movies with Sasha and Baden.

But you'll have Baden all to yourself.

Another voice countered, *Only because Sasha's not around.* Just like the stolen kiss in the pool, Baden would sometimes unexpectedly touch her or kiss her, but only when Sasha was otherwise occupied or absent. Without her having realised it, he'd drawn an invisible line that was only now starting to be visible to her. And yet often when the three of them were together they felt like a family. Uncertainty ran through her.

Stop it! You're over-analysing. She tried to shake off the melancholy that had settled over her by flirting. 'So, do you have a date for this movie?'

'I have a picnic rug, some Irish coffee and Swiss chocolates.' His voice deepened caressingly. 'Would you care to join me?'

Of course you'll join him. His words washed over her, stealing away the tiny squeak of rebellion that had stirred. She let him draw her away from the crowds to a dark and quiet area. Next to his car, in the glow of the fading light, lay a rug covered in cushions and the biggest box of chocolates she'd ever seen.

She tilted her head enquiringly, trying to keep her face straight. 'It's not the best view of the screen—in fact, I doubt whether I'll be able to even see the film.'

His arm swung around her waist, pulling her against him, his heat surging into her. He cupped her cheek with his free hand and stroked her face tenderly with his thumb.

His smile streaked through his five o'clock stubble, dark and deliciously dangerous. His voice, low and husky, rumbled around her. 'Now you're catching on.'

Shimmers of delight raced along her veins as she gazed at him with complete freedom as she'd longed to do all day, losing herself in his smile and everything it promised.

He lowered his mouth against hers, his tongue barely skating across her lips in the softest yet most erotic kiss she'd ever known.

This was where she belonged. She tilted her head back, opened her mouth under his and gave herself up to him.

With the same delicate pressure he roved over her mouth, exploring and tasting every part of it in a slow, deliberate manner, as if he was exploring and tasting every part of her.

She gripped his shoulders for support, her fingers pressing

into solid muscle as her legs lost all power to hold her upright. Languid pleasure rolled through her like the ripple of wind on water, making her ache for more, making her stand perfectly still so she didn't miss a moment.

Time stood still. Colours intensified, her perception of space and place altered as she lost herself in the kiss from the man she loved.

Eventually he lifted his head as the last light faded and the moon rose. 'I've wanted to do that all day.'

Her heart sang. 'Really?'

'Really.' He tucked her hair behind her ear. 'Did you know you're incredibly sexy when you're in organising mode?'

Laughing, she sank down onto the picnic rug and opened the chocolates, suddenly famished. 'I doubt Linton sees me that way, especially when I told him he *had* to be MC. I'm pretty sure he'd say I was just plain bossy.'

Baden sat down next to her with a growl, his hand curving around her thigh in a proprietorial way. 'If Linton was to ever think you're sexy, he would have to contend with me.'

A smile opened up deep inside her, expanding into every part of her, filling her with inexplicable happiness. Baden wanted her just for himself. She hugged that knowledge tightly.

She lay down on the cushions and stretched out, blissfully happy. 'A duel at dawn, perhaps?'

He lay down next to her, his fingers trailing across her almost bare shoulders, toying with the spaghetti straps of her dress. 'Hmm, something like that.' He kissed the hollow at the base of her neck and then gave her a light nip. 'Or perhaps I'll just brand you as mine.'

She laughed and rolled into his arms where she belonged.

He hugged her close. 'I'm planning on us having a *lot* of moments like this in the future.'

A thrill of wonder wove through her. He wanted her *and* they had a future together. This time she'd got it right, this time she'd fallen in love with the right man.

A man with a daughter she adored. Suddenly she'd gone from living alone to a woman with a family. An image of the three of them living together at Sandon filled her head. It felt so very right.

'It sounds perfect to me.' She whispered the words against his mouth and gave herself up to his bone-melting kisses.

Lost in the ministrations of his superb mouth, it took a moment for her to realise that a narrow beam of weak torch-light was suddenly splayed over them. Giggles and shrieks sounded from the bushes behind them.

Baden immediately stilled, his lips sliding away from hers.

'Isn't that Sasha's dad kissing Koala?' a young girl's voice asked in a loud whisper.

The beam of light suddenly veered sideways, as if someone had grabbed the torch. 'Shh, they might hear you. Come on, we have to get back before Dad misses us.'

Kate recognised Phoebe Walton's voice and started to chuckle. 'I think we've just been sprung.'

Baden sat up, his body rigid. 'Hell. What if they tell Sasha?'

Kate pushed herself up and sat beside him, taking his hand in hers. 'If they do, it's no big deal.'

'No big deal?' He ran his free hand across the back of his neck. 'I didn't want her to find out this way.'

Kate shrugged. 'I agree it's not ideal but you can tell her in the morning or, better yet, *we* can tell her together after the film.'

'Tell her?' His bewildered expression made her smile. He looked like a little boy who'd just got lost. 'I wasn't planning on telling her anything.'

She frowned, surprised by his comment and suddenly

feeling a bit bewildered herself. 'Do you really think that's wise, not telling her?'

Disbelief showed on his face. 'I don't know about you, but I don't expect my twelve-year-old to understand an affair. And that's what we're having, right? What we both want. No relationship, no ties, but some time together.' He reached for her. 'Just the two of us.'

Her stomach rolled and she gagged as his words pounded her. *I'm planning on us having a lot of moments like this in the future.*

Oh, God, he meant clandestine moments. Stolen times like now and in Dog Tired Hut. Times without Sasha. Times Sasha would not know about.

He had no intention of making her part of his family. He and Sasha were the family. She was only a bit of fluff on the side.

Her world, so perfect a few moments ago, imploded— caving in on her with suffocating reality. She pushed his hands away and found her voice. 'You might have been talking about an affair but I certainly wasn't.'

The lines on his forehead deepened. 'But you said it sounded perfect. What did you think I was talking about?'

She tossed her head high, trying to hold on to her shredded dignity. 'I thought you were talking about a future together. You, me and Sasha.'

A stunned expression crossed his face. 'But you told me you didn't want another relationship.'

She stood up, wringing her hands as her own words came back to bite her. 'I know I told you that and at the time it was the truth, but things change.'

He'd risen to his feet and now leaned against the car. 'We can't be together. I have to do what's best for Sasha. Surely you understand that.' His troubled gaze appealed to her for understanding.

Her brain struggled to make sense of what he was saying. 'No, I'm sorry, I really don't understand how not moving forward with your life is better for Sasha.'

His expression hardened. 'Sasha needs my total attention and I can't allow anything or anyone to get in the way of that. At least, not until she's an adult.'

His words stung like salt on a wound. 'But it's OK to have sex with me once a month while she visits her grandparents in Adelaide?'

He flinched and she knew her words had hit the target with pinpoint accuracy. Obviously that had been his plan. A convenient affair.

He ploughed his hand through his hair. 'You're making it sound sordid and you know it isn't like that at all.'

Anger fizzed in her veins. 'Well, forgive me if I don't see it quite the way you do.' She breathed in deeply, trying to slow her pounding heart. His line of thinking was illogical.

She formed her thoughts carefully. 'Baden, you and Sasha have the most amazing relationship and I would never, ever want to come between you or change what you have.'

Relief flooded his face. 'Which is why my plan will work so well for us.'

Her heart tore, the ripping reverberating through her. He had no idea what she meant. She shook her head. 'Your plan is not going to work. Your plan denies Sasha everything she needs. Your plan locks your daughter into this unhealthy cloister of an existence. You're denying her a chance of a normal family life, to be part of a loving family, to have brothers and sisters and pets.'

She mustered every ounce of courage she had and hauled her gaze to his. 'Over the last few months I've fallen in love with you and your wonderful Sasha. I want to create a family with you, to give Sasha the chance to be a big sister.'

His look of horror was like a knife through her heart.

'Oh, hell.' He started to pace. 'Oh, Kate, I had no idea.' He spoke quietly, his eyes full of contrition. 'I made a promise to Annie that Sasha would always come first and I plan to honour that.'

She swayed as if she'd been hit. How could she compete against a dead wife who stood between them? She closed her eyes for a brief moment, hoping to steel her legs into holding her up for just a bit longer. Sasha's words about her mother played through her mind. From what she'd gleaned, Annie had been a loving, sensible and wonderful mother. She didn't sound like a selfish woman who had feared losing her daughter's love after death.

'Did she really mean that you couldn't love again?'

His eyes flickered with emotion, but sadness illuminated them most strongly. Sadness for her.

The truth suddenly rushed in with all the devastating power of a tsunami.

He didn't love her.

Pain like she'd never known travelled through her, searing her, scarring her, sapping every particle of joy and happiness from her soul. Blackness seeped in, staining her with misery.

'Time for bed, Sash.' Baden dropped a light kiss on his daughter's head.

Freshly showered and dressed in her pink pyjamas, a yawning and exhausted Sasha snuggled up to him on the couch, her head against his chest. 'My brain's all spinning around though, Dad. I don't think I'll be able to get to sleep.'

'Once you're in bed, you'll soon go to sleep.' His words sounded false to his ears. He knew he'd be lying awake, thinking about tonight. Thinking about Kate. Hell, what a mess.

Never in a million years had he expected her to fall in love with him. He hated it that he'd hurt her so much but he couldn't give her what she wanted. He had to take the safe path through life for Sasha's sake.

'Tonight was the best night I've ever had.' Sasha looked up, her eyes shining. 'Wasn't Kate awesome? She and I had so much fun selling the food, and the movie was a crack-up.' She paused for a beat and then tickled him. 'That means funny, Dad.'

He raised his brows. 'And here I was thinking the film was, like, totally random.'

'Ha-ha, Dad—not.' She smiled to herself. 'When the first movie finished, we all pummelled Mr Walton with foam and sat on him until he bought us ice creams. It was cool and I can't wait to visit Sandon tomorrow and tell Kate all about it.'

He tried to sound casually matter-of-fact. 'We won't be seeing Kate tomorrow.'

Sasha pushed herself up, her expression one large question mark. 'Why not? We've visited her most days lately.'

Because I've hurt her deeply. Because she won't want to see me again. Kate's huge brown eyes filled with anguish haunted him. He breathed in deeply, thinking carefully. Sasha must never know what had gone on between him and Kate; she wouldn't understand.

'The fundraiser's over now, Sash, and we won't be visiting Sandon again.' He kept his voice even. 'Go on, now, off to bed and I'll be there in a minute to tuck you in.'

Sasha stayed put, her mouth taking on a mulish look. 'But she invited me over and I want to go.'

He stroked her hair. 'I know you and Kate did some special things these last few weeks but that's finished now. You'll still see her at Guides on Wednesdays.'

'Why are you being so mean?' Sasha unexpectedly pushed her finger into his chest.

He wrapped his hand around hers, stopping the jabbing, trying to keep calm. 'I am *not* being mean. I'm just pointing out that all good things come to an end and life goes back to normal. Kate's busy with work and Guides and she doesn't need you taking up her time.'

'But she's my special friend. She understands stuff.'

Her expression told him she clearly thought he didn't understand stuff and she mumbled something.

'Pardon?' His tone demanded she repeat it.

A defiant look streaked across her face. 'I said she's like a mum, except different.'

Like a mum. The words sank into him, exposing a set of emotions he didn't want to explore. Sasha had *him*, that had to be enough.

'She's your Guide leader, Sasha, and you can see her there.' He heard the thread of impatience in his voice.

Sasha suddenly looked coy. 'Phoebe Walton said she saw you kissing and cuddling Kate so that makes her your special friend, too.' Sasha was like a dog with a bone. He'd never seen her this determined or intense. Her eyes shone with hope and she wheedled, 'That makes her *our* special friend, doesn't it, Dad? And you visit special friends.'

The room suddenly seemed airless as the walls pressed in on him. He went into damage control. 'Phoebe must have seen me giving Kate a quick thank-you kiss. That doesn't make her a special friend. She's my work colleague and my flight nurse and that's all.'

You keep telling yourself that, mate.

He blocked the voice out of his head. He was a father and it was time to start acting like one. 'I'm sorry but you can't go and see Kate at Sandon any more, and that's the end of the discussion.' He gave her a gentle nudge. 'Now, go to bed.'

Sasha launched herself off the couch, tears streaming down her flushed and angry face. 'I hate you, Dad, I hate you so much!' She turned and ran, her bare feet pummelling the polished boards in the hall. A moment later her bedroom door slammed, setting all the windows vibrating.

Hell. What was it with the women in his life tonight?

You're the problem. He stood up and walked over to his CD player, turning on some quiet music to drown out the voice in his head.

As much as Sasha and Kate hated him right now, he knew what was best for him and Sasha. He had to stick to his plan. It was all he had. It was the only safe thing he could depend on. Annie had died. Kate could decide she didn't love Sasha after all and leave. He wasn't going to risk his daughter's happiness when there were no absolute certainties.

But why did being in the right have to be so damn lonely?

The grandfather clock chimed two. Baden looked up from the glow of the computer screen, last year's tax figures blurring in front of his eyes. Kate and then Sasha had sent his brain into overdrive so there'd been no point going to bed. Instead, he'd tackled his overdue tax figures. At least his accountant would be pleased with him.

He's about the only person who will be.

Snapping down the top of his laptop, he cleared the cups off the table, dumping them in the sink. Walking down the hall, he paused outside Sasha's room. Usually he tucked her in even if she'd been moody, but with tonight's exhaustion-induced tantrum, he hadn't gone in, thinking it wiser to wait until she was asleep.

In the morning, when she wasn't exhausted any more, he'd suggest she visit Erin and together they could rehash the events of the drive-in night, as girls liked to do. That would satisfy her and Kate would recede to being the Guide leader.

He quietly opened the bedroom door. He never went to bed without peeking in on Sasha. The day may have been a beast but she always looked angelic in sleep and his heart filled with the joy she gave him.

The glow from the moon came through the open window. He was surprised the window was fully open. He crept over and slowly dropped the sash halfway into its usual position and then lowered the Roman blind. Sasha needed a good eleven hours' sleep and the sun rose early.

As usual the room was a jumble of clothes, books, CDs and open dressing-table drawers, with clothes spilling out of them. What was it with not being able to open *and* close a drawer? He bent down to pick up the pink quilt, which had slid to the floor. As he stood up he caught sight of the bed. It was empty.

Without thinking, he reached out and put his hand on the bottom sheet. Cold.

He swung back to the window as fear slithered through him. The window was never wide open like it had been. Surely Sasha hadn't crawled out and run away?

The clothes she'd been wearing at the drive-in were still on a heap on the floor. Perhaps she hadn't gone very far.

He strode out into the hall. 'Sasha? Sweetheart, are you here?' He opened every door in the house, calling her name, each time sounding more frantic than before.

He tugged open the hall cupboard, grabbed the torch and ran out the back door. 'Sasha!' He swung the torch around the garden and scanned the tree house.

She wasn't there.

He sprinted around the side of the house to her bedroom window. A bush with a few broken and flattened branches declared Sasha had left the house.

Panic flooded him and chaotic thoughts ricocheted around his brain. His twelve-year-old daughter was out in the dark, alone. His throat constricted.

Think! He started to pace. She was upset so where would she have gone? Erin lived three streets away. He belted inside and grabbed the phone, his fingers thumping the numbers hard and fast. *Pick up, pick up.* He willed the Baxters to hear the ring, and have it wake them from their slumber.

The ringing stopped and a clunking noise sounded before a sleepy voice came down the line. 'Hello. James Baxter.'

He breathed out slowly so that he didn't gabble. 'James, Baden Tremont. Sorry to bother you but Sasha's missing. Is she with you? She might have sneaked into Erin's room.'

There was a short silence, as if James was digesting the request. 'Right, I'll go and check for you, but I think you'd better speak to Trix.'

Erin's mother came on the line. 'Baden, what's wrong?'

He sighed. 'Sasha and I had an argument and she's run away. You're the closest house so I thought she might be with you.' He heard James's voice murmuring in the background.

'James says Erin's asleep and there's no sign of Sasha.' She paused for a moment. 'Think about the argument—that might give you a clue to where she's gone.'

Kate.

'Thanks, Trix, you're brilliant. I'll call you back.'

He scribbled a note. 'I love you, Sasha. Ring me on my mobile if you're reading this.' Grabbing his car keys, he left the front and back doors unlocked and reversed the car down the drive.

He drove slowly all the way to Kate's, his lights on high beam, hoping to see a small figure walking along the road. Shadows jumped out at him but they were shadows of his imagination.

She must be at Kate's. She had to be at Kate's.

Of course she would be at Kate's.

He turned into Sandon's long curving drive, the tall cypress trees lining the road casting moonlight shadows on the gravel. Rupert started barking as soon as he stepped out of the car.

'Shh, Rupe, it's just me.'

Veranda lights sensed his movement and illuminated the thick oak front door. Panic made him pound on it. 'Kate, answer the door.'

A moment later her anxious voice came from the other side of the screen door. 'Baden? Is that you?'

Hell, he'd scared her. 'Yes, it's me.'

He heard her sharp intake of breath before she opened the door. Dark rings hovered under her eyes, which stared at him in wariness as she tied a dressing-gown around her.

'Have you been drinking? It's two o'clock in the morning.' Her arctic tone told him he wasn't welcome, that his unexpected arrival had brought scarring memories back.

He hated himself for doing this to her, but he couldn't deal with that right now. Right now only Sasha mattered and his fear for his daughter did away with any preliminaries. He pushed past her, opening doors, looking left and right.

'What are you doing?' She pulled his arm. 'Baden, what's going on?'

Guilt almost choked him. He couldn't hurt Kate any further by telling her that he'd told his daughter she couldn't come and visit her. 'She was overtired after the drive-in, we had an argument and she's run away.' He started to pace. 'She's not at the Baxters', and I doubt she'd be at the Waltons' so I thought she might be here.'

Silently Kate stared at him, her large eyes filled with astonishment and then fear.

A shiver ran across his skin and his chest tightened. At that moment he knew with dazzling clarity that, no matter how much he'd hurt Kate, if Sasha had come to Sandon, she would have telephoned him immediately. She would put Sasha ahead of how she felt about him, no matter how much he'd hurt her.

She opened her mouth. 'What was the arg—' She stopped, breathed in and her expression changed from shock to crisis planning. When she spoke again she was all business. 'How long do you think she might have been gone for?'

'It was eleven when she went to bed.' The words sounded stark in the darkness. 'She could have been gone as long as three hours.'

A look of horror rolled across her face on hearing about the elapsed time. 'Surely if she was with one of her friends, their parents would have rung you.' She started to walk toward the kitchen. 'Oh, but then again the girl she fled to might be hiding her because they're both scared that you or her parents would be angry.'

A glimmer of relief sparked inside him. 'You're right, I never thought of that. I'll start ringing.' He pulled out his mobile.

'Hang on. You need to do this systematically.' She rummaged through her sideboard cupboard and pulled out a manila folder of phone numbers. 'This is the Guides' contact list. Take it and start ringing from your house in case Sasha has returned or is about to return. Mark off each name as you phone so you don't miss anyone.'

Her sensible words started to break through his fog of fear. Thank goodness he'd come here. Kate was the most amazing woman he'd ever met. 'Good idea.'

She picked up her mobile phone, checking the display. 'I've

got a full battery and I'll have this in my pocket all the time I'm driving around town looking for her. Contact me any time. Better yet, ring me after an hour, unless one of us finds her before the hour is up.'

She put her hand on his arm. 'We'll find her.'

Her warmth seeped into him, soothing and reassuring at a time he thought those feelings to be impossible. He covered her hand with his. 'Thanks, Kate. I really appreciate your help.'

She jerkily pulled her hand out from under his. 'I'm doing it for Sasha.'

Her words sliced through him. He knew he didn't deserve her sympathy and understanding, but it hurt more than he'd anticipated.

He nodded and walked to the patio door.

'Baden.'

He turned at the sombre tone of her voice.

'If you draw a blank, you *must* ring Daryl Thornton at the police station. As soon as it's first light, a search can be started.'

She voiced the thoughts that he'd held at bay for the last hour.

Jagged fear ripped through him, sucking his breath from his lungs. Where the hell was his beautiful daughter?

CHAPTER ELEVEN

KATE pulled on her jeans, thick hiking socks, a long-sleeved T-shirt and a polar fleece. If this turned into a full-on search and rescue then she was going to be prepared. Daryl Thornton, the police sergeant, would shoot her otherwise. Good preparation was vital and he'd drilled it into all the members of the emergency service.

When she'd heard Baden's pounding on the door every nightmare of Shane coming home drunk had rushed through her. Why would he be on her doorstep sober? He'd told her to her face that he didn't love her so there was no reason for him to visit.

But the moment she'd seen him standing on her veranda, his face ashen under the yellow light, his hair standing up on end from being ploughed through by agitated fingers, she'd known something was desperately wrong. His blue eyes had been stark as he'd stared through her as if searching beyond her.

And she understood completely.

Sasha was missing. Sasha, whom she loved like a daughter. What had possessed her to take off in the middle of the night?

She stowed medical gear into her backpack, filled her water bottle, packed some sustenance bars and headed out to the car.

If Sasha hadn't been found by dawn, she was all prepared to join the official search, which Daryl wouldn't start until then.

Meanwhile, she'd start her town search at the school, although she doubted Sasha would have gone there. Her head-lights swept the streets, which were eerily empty, as they usually were a few hours before daybreak. She searched the school, the bus depot, the Guide Hall, the pool—all the places in town that were familiar to Sasha.

But she found nothing. No sign of Sasha.

Where would she have gone? She banged her head against the steering-wheel. *Think like a girl.*

Her brain was grey fog. She stared through the windscreen at the green road sign displaying names of places out of town.

Sasha's sweet voice sounded in her head. *Once I walked from home to Ledger's Gorge. I really liked it there, it was a good place to think, you know?*

If you'd had an argument with your father, you'd need to think. Ledger's Gorge was a decent walk in daylight. It would be almost impossible in pitch darkness. The arguments went around in her head. Still, it was the best shot she had. She started the car and headed out of town.

The only sign of habitation at the Ledger's Gorge picnic spot were two wombats grazing in the moonlight. Kate got out of the car, cupped her hands around her mouth and yelled into the darkness. 'Sash-a.'

She held her breath, wishing for a reply. All she got was an echo of her own voice.

She swung her high-beam torch around the area. It illumi-nated the carved wooden sign that marked the start of the steep walk down to the gorge. Even in daylight it was a tricky walk. Surely Sasha wouldn't have gone down there?

The crazy thought took hold, niggling her until she couldn't ignore it any longer. She strapped on her backpack, put her mobile phone in her pocket, gripped her torch and started to walk along the narrow and rough track. Every ten steps she called out Sasha's name and waited, her ears straining for a reply.

Twigs snapped underfoot, making her jump. *Go back, no kid would do this in the dark.* But Sasha could be determined, almost as determined as her father, and for some reason Kate couldn't rule this crazy venture out of her head.

She reached the top of the steep and narrow steps that were carved out of the red rock. She gingerly took the first step. *One down, ninety-nine to go.* 'Sasha!'

Her voice came back to her. Then she thought she heard a small sound. She held her breath.

Silence.

She lowered herself onto the next overly large step and slid her bottom along it, the darkness making her feel dizzy. This was why they didn't do search and rescue in the dark. *But this is Sasha.* She managed another ten steps that way.

'Sasha!' She swung her torch in an arc, squinting to see any sign of anything that wasn't a tree. One side was blackness, the side that fell to the gorge only black space between her and the bottom.

At step forty-seven she decided she was the one who was crazy, unwise and foolhardy. If Sasha was here, she would have heard her calls by now. *Go back to town.* She stood up and gave one more almighty yell, shining the torch from side to side and down.

The white light cut through the darkness, catching a flash of colour. She moved it back. Pink. She blinked in disbelief. Below her she could see pink. 'Sasha.'

But the pink didn't move.

Her heart hammered wildly in her chest as she sat down and

bottom-shuffled another fifteen steps. She shone her torch. On a ledge just below the stairs, cushioned in thick bush, lay Sasha's inert body clad in pink pyjamas.

Be alive. Be alive. She scrambled to the edge, and shone the torch. The drop from the steps wasn't much more than six feet. *You can get down there without a harness.* Somehow she managed to lower herself down, her feet finding footholds, her fingernails digging into the crevices, until she dropped the last bit.

Prickly branches scratched her as she tumbled onto the ledge. She took in a deep breath and wriggled. Everything moved, nothing hurt. She crawled slowly to Sasha and immediately pulled her away from the edge of the ledge.

Gently shaking her shoulder, she tried to rouse her. 'Sasha, sweetheart, it's Kate.'

The girl's eyelashes fluttered open and closed again.

Thank you, thank you. She sent up a prayer. She shone the torch on Sasha's face. Blood had clotted at her temple and her face was badly scratched by the bushes. She checked her airway and breathing, then gently opened each eyelid and tested her pupils. The black discs contracted. At least she could rule out a brain injury.

'Sasha, I'm going to see if you have done yourself any more damage.'

The girl moaned as Kate systematically ran her hands down Sasha's arms and then her legs, feeling for misalignment, pretty much dependent on her sense of touch rather than sight as she juggled the torch in her mouth.

A sob broke from Sasha's lips as Kate's hands pressed on her lower left leg, which lay at an angle.

'I'm sorry, Sash. You've broken your leg.'

The young girl started to cry, the pain from her leg seeming to have jolted her back to consciousness. 'Oh, Kate, I was so scared. Daddy's going to kill me.'

Kate stroked her temple and kissed her forehead. 'Shh, no, he's not. He's going to be thrilled you're safe.' She pulled out a space blanket and tucked it around Sasha to keep her warm. 'I'm going to ring him now and when the sun comes up he'll be here to take you to hospital.'

She set the torch securely in the fork of a bush and pulled out her phone. Leaning in close to the torch, she auto-dialled Baden's mobile and then put the phone to her ear.

The sound of ringing never started.

She held the phone under the beam of light. The signal detector was blank. Her heart slammed against her chest. *You idiot!* She was so used to using her work satellite phone she'd never even thought that her mobile phone wouldn't work out here.

She was stuck on a ledge, with a child with a concussion and a fractured leg, and no way of getting any help.

Daryl would string her up and ditch her from the search and rescue squad.

Baden would never forgive her.

'So what do you think she was wearing when she left home?'

Daryl opened his spiral-bound notepad as he stood in the middle of Sasha's room.

Baden tried to pull his fried brain together. 'She's got a lot of clothes but I've looked through them and I think the only things missing are her pink pyjamas and her walking boots. The lantern torch is gone but her backpack is still here.'

'It's cold out there tonight. Would she have a jacket?'

Baden opened the drawer where Sasha stored her hoodies and polar fleeces, his hands riffling through the contents, trying to keep his thoughts calm enough to think. 'Perhaps a red hoodie, but I'm not certain.' In thin pink pyjamas, hypothermia was a real concern. Regret slashed him. Sasha was out there somewhere, alone and cold, and it was all his fault.

'And you've rung her friends, you say, and no one's seen her?' The fatherly policeman's bushy eyebrows rose in question.

Baden pulled his mind back to the details. 'That's right and Kate Lawson has been doing a town search while I did the ring around from here in case Sasha came home.'

'Wise idea. Well, she's been gone five hours now so I'll put the call out to our volunteer searchers. We'll meet at the station in an hour.'

'I'll be there.' Relief flooded him that he could finally do something more tangible to look for Sasha.

Daryl flipped his notebook closed. 'Doc, someone has to be here at the house in case she does come home under her own steam.'

'I can't sit around here any longer. I have to do something.' His voice rose in frustration.

Daryl scratched his head. 'The kiddie knows Kate, doesn't she? Ring her and get her back here. She can man the house and that frees you up to search. I'll see you at the briefing.'

'Right, I'll be there.'

Sasha, be safe, please, be safe. I promised to keep you safe.

The moment Daryl left the house, Baden dialled Kate's number. 'The number you have telephoned is either turned off or out of range. Please try again later.' The recorded message droned on. In his haste he must have dialled the wrong number. He tried again but this time he used the number already listed in the contacts list to avoid a mistake.

The same message played.

I've got a full battery and I'll have this in my pocket all the time I'm driving around town, looking for her.

He glanced at the clock. He'd missed the check-in phone call because he'd been with Daryl. His unease ramped up. Kate wouldn't have turned off her phone. She was experienced in search and rescue and she knew the vital importance of communication. He knew she would have rung him when she hadn't heard from him.

His stomach curdled. Something was wrong. Very wrong. The only reason she wouldn't have rung him was if she wasn't able to. If something serious had happened to her.

An insidious thought edged though him, taking hold. Two females missing. Shocking things, unmentionable things sometimes happened in small towns as well as in big ones.

His blood turned to ice as his fear for Sasha, already at breaking point, compounded with his dread for Kate. He collapsed into a chair, dropping his head into his hands. First he'd lost Sasha, now Kate was missing. What if he lost them both?

Crushing pain bore down on his chest, sending silver spots wavering before his eyes. He couldn't lose either of them. He couldn't lose his daughter and the woman he loved.

The woman he loved.

He loved her. He dragged in a ragged breath. Oh, God, he'd been such a fool. He'd got it all wrong. His promise to make Sasha his top priority didn't mean he couldn't love again. It meant he should love a woman who loved Sasha. A woman Sasha loved, too.

Kate was that woman and he'd pushed her and her love away.

Now she was missing and he couldn't tell her he loved her. And that Sasha loved her, too.

Move! a voice roared in his head. *Go!*

He had to find the two most important people in his life. He had to find them, hold them and tell them he loved them both.

He rang Daryl as he ran to the car. 'Kate's missing, too. I want the helicopter brought in and I'll be on it.'

* * *

Kate's fingers burned from cold as she checked Sasha's pulse. It was rapid but that could be due to pain. The birds started to twitter, their cacophony of sound heralding the rise of the sun. A large red ball, it rose from behind the gorge, banishing the dark and bringing much-needed warmth.

At any other time the beauty would have awed her but not today. She'd spent the last hour cuddling Sasha close, using her own body heat to warm the frightened child and the space blanket to trap the heat around them.

The unforgiving rock and dirt had dug into her hip while the bushes poked her. She'd never complain about her mattress again. Sasha had slept fitfully in between being woken up for head-injury observations.

Kate sighed. At least she knew that Baden would have contacted Daryl and a search would be getting into full swing. But they would start searching from Baden's house and move out in concentric rings. Did Baden know Sasha loved the peace of the gorge? Had she ever told him she liked to come here to think?

They could be here for hours. Why, why hadn't she rung Baden to tell him she was heading out this way before she'd left town? But hindsight was a wonderful thing. She chewed her lip. At least her car was in the car park if someone from town thought to come out here and made the connection.

'Kate.' Sasha gripped her hand and started to sob. 'It really hurts. When are they coming to get me?'

Her stomach sank but she couldn't lie. 'Honey, I don't know. But you need to use some of that bravery that made you walk out here in the dark alone.'

A small voice replied, 'I don't think it was bravery. I think it was probably stupidity.'

Kate gave a wry smile. 'Perhaps, but sometimes when we're angry or sad we don't think things through very well.'

Sasha nodded. 'I was so angry with Dad. I wanted to come out to see you at Sandon this morning and he said I would only be seeing you at Guides.'

Kate's heart sank. The one person she and Baden wanted to protect most had ended up getting hurt. 'Well, you're seeing me now and when you're all tucked up in a hospital bed we'll talk to your dad about you coming to visit me now and then. I don't think he realised it was quite so important to you.'

Or to me.

If Baden hadn't been able to share Sasha before, he certainly wouldn't be able to now. The fear of losing her would only make him hold her closer and push Kate further and further away. Not that there was any room left to push. He'd left her in no doubt—he didn't love her. The bleak thought chilled her as much as the dawn air.

She reached for her medical bag now that the light was bright enough to see by. She gasped as she caught sight of the precipitous drop a mere ten metres away from where they lay. She didn't want to think about what could have happened if the bushes hadn't broken Sasha's fall.

'Sasha, I'm going to examine you again now I can see and put in an IV so I can give you something for the pain.'

'Will it hurt?' Sasha shivered under the silver space blanket.

'Not compared to falling off those steps.' She slipped the tourniquet around Sasha's arm. 'Your job is to look upwards toward the steps and see if you can see anyone. We'll start calling out in an hour when there might be a chance a tourist is visiting.'

'OK.' Sasha flinched as the cannula went into her arm.

Kate attached the five hundred millilitre bag of saline to the cannula and hung it from a tree. Then she pulled her polar fleece over her head. 'I'm going to take off your pink PJ top and you can wear this.'

'Why?'

'Your fluoro pink top is really bright and I'm going to spread it out on top of this bush. Then if we hear or see anything, I'll wave it over my head.'

'And the rescuers will see it because it isn't green like the trees or red like the dirt.'

'Exactly.' She gave Sasha a reassuring stroke of the head. 'I found you because of this pink so they'll find us, too.' *I hope.*

'And Dad said I had too much pink.' Sasha tried to laugh but grimaced in pain.

Kate splinted Sasha's leg, giving thanks it wasn't a compound fracture. She didn't need a bone sticking out through skin in this dirt. The sun rose higher in the sky and every five minutes she called out, "Coo-ee! Help!"

The only response she got was a visit by geckos and skinks, the tiny lizards that hid in the crevices, who came out on the rocks to sun themselves. She took a slug of water from her drink bottle, munched on a sustenance bar and waited.

Sasha moved abruptly.

'What's wrong? Does it hurt somewhere new?' Kate was instantly alert.

'No. Listen.' Sasha stared up. 'Can you hear that noise?'

A faint whirring sounded in the distance. *A plane.*

Kate struggled to her feet and grabbed the pink pyjama top, shoving a long stick through the arm.

The whirring grew louder. 'Will they see us?' Anxiety vibrated from Sasha as she squinted into the sky.

'I hope so, sweetie, and then they'll tell the rescuers where to come.' Kate raised the stick over her head.

A yellow helicopter suddenly appeared above the red cliffs, banked and flew up the gorge.

'Wave it, Kate, wave it,' Sasha yelled above the deafening noise of the rotors of the approaching helicopter.

With feet planted wide apart she waved the pink pyjama flag high over her head in an arc, back and forth, as if she were signalling the end of a Grand Prix race, praying the occupants of the helicopter would see it.

The helicopter flew past, the noise receding as it rose up out of the gorge.

Kate lowered the stick. 'They should fly round again, Sasha.' *Please, please, see us.*

'It's getting louder.' Sasha craned her neck, trying to see.

The muscles in Kate's arms screamed but she raised the flag again and started waving it. The helicopter approached more slowly this time. Her breath caught in her throat. Had they seen her?

The helicopter inched closer, until it hovered close to them, the noise deafening as dirt and dust swirled from the updraught of the rotors.

She caught sight of Baden's face, white with relief and fear.

She gave a thumbs-up, hoping to ease his fright. She yelled to Sasha, 'Your dad's just found us, sweetheart.'

Sasha gave a watery smile.

The helicopter rose and turned, positioning itself over them, the pilot skilfully hovering, not moving the chopper an inch from its position. An electric winch lowered a container onto the ledge. Kate grabbed it and opened it up to find a two-way radio.

'Kate do you read me, over?' Baden's reassuring but strained voice rumbled through the speaker.

Relief rushed through her. 'I read you loud and clear, Baden.

Sasha is safe. She has a suspected fractured tib and fib and a slight concussion but she's conscious and alert. Over.'

'Thank God. I'm coming down, over.' The relief in his voice was palpable.

Above her, Baden, dressed in bright orange emergency services clothing and a hard hat, connected his harness to the steel line, which was lowered toward her. As his hips came within arm's reach, she steadied his descent until his feet touched the ground.

His arms wrapped around her for an infinitesimal moment, their pressure reassuring and wonderful. Then he stepped back and a sense of loss hit her.

'Strap your radio to your body.' His command came through the radio so he could be heard over the noise of the helicopter.

The doctor in charge had arrived. There was a job to be done and he was reminding her of her role in the rescue. Failed co-worker. Her heart, already torn and bruised, broke a little more.

He moved away from her and dropped down next to his daughter, stark relief and love shinning from his eyes as Sasha reached up and wrapped her arms around his neck.

Kate bit her lip. Father and daughter reunited—as it should be. She hated the cold and heavy emptiness that dragged through her at the knowledge that she couldn't be part of this reunion.

He motioned for her to bob down on the other side of Sasha so the patient and the pilot could hear both radios.

Baden checked the air splint on Sasha's leg. 'Has she had any pain relief?'

Kate nodded. 'An hour ago.'

'Great. Thanks.' He lowered his head to Sasha. 'I need you to be really, really brave. I'm going to put you into the harness and hug you against me. Your leg might hurt but it's the best way to get you out of here. Together we'll be winched back to the helicopter and James will pull us on board.'

'I can do it, Daddy.' Sasha turned to Kate, seeking confirmation. 'Can't I, Kate?'

Her battered heart took another pummelling. 'You can do whatever you put your mind to, sweetheart.' Kate squeezed her hand. 'And in a few hours, after your leg is all plastered, you'll be sipping blue heaven milkshakes in hospital and thinking this was all a bad dream.'

'Will you bring Kate up, too, Daddy?'

Baden shook his head, his shuttered gaze catching Kate's. 'No. Kate will go out on foot.'

Of course she would. She wasn't injured and there were other medical personnel present. But none of that knowledge stopped a lump forming in her throat.

She flicked into work mode. Pushing away every personal feeling she had, she supported Sasha while Baden's strong and steady hands fitted the harness. Together they positioned Sasha against Baden and he crossed his legs over Sasha's to hug her against him then gave the signal to James.

The winch started to wind. Kate watched as the two people she loved most in the world moved upwards and away from her.

The tears she'd been holding back for twelve hours spilled over.

Kate's head pounded. Daryl had harangued her from the moment he'd dropped the rope ladder down to her so she could climb off the ledge, he'd berated her as she'd walked up the fifty steps back to the car park and he'd lectured her as he'd driven her to Warragurra Base Hospital. Then he'd hugged her, thanked her and left her sitting in A and E drinking hot tea.

'Warming up now?' Linton stuck his head into the doctors' lounge. He smiled his playboy grin. 'I hear you're being a difficult patient and have refused to sit in a cubicle.'

She rolled her eyes. 'That would be because I'm *not* a

patient. I'm fine. Nothing that a hot shower and some sleep won't cure.' She warmed her hands around the mug as she rested back in the soft couch. 'Besides, I look in better shape than you do. Big night last night, was it?'

He looked sheepish as he spun a chair out from under a table and sat astride it. 'I was merely being a good host as you'd instructed, and after the drive-in I introduced the newly arrived physio students to Warragurra's night life.'

Her tea almost spurted out of her mouth. 'I only asked you to be the MC.' She gave him a long look. 'So now you've dated every nurse at the hospital, you're moving on to students? Don't you think they're a bit young for you?'

For a moment he looked affronted but then his expression smoothed into its usual urbane lines and he teased her. 'Hey, you and I haven't dated. I promise a fun time.'

She laughed. 'And a don't-call-me,-I'll-call-you policy. Thank you, but I think I'll pass.'

He stood up and swung the chair back under the table, his eyes dark with understanding. 'Sasha Tremont is out of Theatre after a straightforward reduction and internal fixation of her left leg and she's ready for visitors.'

'Thanks, Linton.' She ran her finger around the rim of the cup. Baden would be with her. She hadn't seen him since he'd been winched away. 'I'll visit her a bit later. Hope A and E isn't too busy for you today.'

He grinned and disappeared back to the action.

She should go home and have a shower. She should tie up all the loose ends after the drive-in. She should plan next week's Guide activity. She should do a million things.

But inertia claimed her and she just sat there.

The door clicked open and she glanced up from her thoughts. 'Linton said you were here.' Baden's hoarse voice spoke quietly. He looked like hell. His curls lay flat after being jammed under a hard hat and dark stubble covered his jaw while black smudges ringed his eyes—testament to the raw fear he'd lived with through the night.

She smothered her overwhelming desire to wrap her arms around him and tell him it was over now. Guilt immediately surfaced, turning inside her. Four hours of his fear she could have alleviated if she'd planned before going to the gorge.

He sat down next to her. 'Sasha's asleep.'

She nodded, feeling the tension between them. 'That's the best thing for her.'

'Yeah, it was one hell of night.'

His sigh shuddered through him and she felt some of his dread as the memories came back.

Unspoken words spouted from her mouth. 'I'm so sorry I didn't tell you I was going to the gorge. I could only think of Sasha and I'm so used to the satellite phone...'

His blue eyes glittered when her words stalled. No matter what she said, he'd never forgive her.

'Don't you *ever* do anything so stupid ever again.'

His harsh words slapped her hard, their sting sharp and tingling.

She could understand his anger. She tossed her head to try and maintain her composure. She just had to keep it together a little bit longer.

Suddenly his hands rested on her shoulders, his fingers digging into her skin, almost shaking her. 'Do you hear me? I never, ever want to feel like that again.'

A tickle of fear skated along her veins and then he pulled her hard against his chest, his arms vice-like around her. She could feel his heart pounding against her own.

'What a crazy, stupid, wonderful thing you did, haring off into the bush to find Sasha. But you could have plunged off those steps and missed the ledge.' His voice rose with distress. 'You could have died.'

'But I didn't.' She spoke softly, needing to reassure him, needing to reassure herself.

He gently cupped her face with his hands and stared into her eyes, his own filled with emotion. 'When I couldn't contact you, I thought that some crazed person had abducted you and Sasha. I thought I'd lost you for ever and all I could think was that you were gone and you didn't know that I love you.'

I love you.

Her breath whooshed from her lungs and her brain seized, trying to make sense of his words. 'You love me?' She couldn't hide the bewilderment in her voice.

He dropped his hands from her face, folding his hands over hers, holding them tight. 'I love you with every part of me.'

She wanted so desperately to believe him, to be in his arms, but she didn't understand what was going on. She pulled her hands free and stood up, wrapping her arms around herself to prevent her shaking. 'Last night you told me you couldn't love me. That you'd made a promise and we couldn't be together.'

'I've been such a fool, Kate.' He stood up and walked toward her, his face full of regret. He tried to reach for her but she spun out of his reach, needing the physical distance from him so she could order her thoughts.

He stood still. 'My world was rocked when Annie died and all I could think of was if I lived my life how we had planned, if I kept things the same, then that would give Sasha the security she needed so she could grow up feeling safe.' He ploughed his hand through his hair.

'But life doesn't stand still, does it?' She knew that only too well.

He shook his head. 'No, it doesn't. Sasha realised that before

I did but I was blind to her many attempts at pointing it out. And blind to yours.' He sighed. 'I thought that the promise I made meant never falling in love again and that would keep Sasha safe from being hurt. But that wasn't what it meant at all and all I've done, as you so succinctly put it, is deny her a full and happy life.' He gripped the back of a chair. 'She loves you, Kate.'

She bit her lip and asked the hardest question of her life. 'Is that why you love me, because Sasha does?'

'No!' The word exploded over her as he strode to her side. He gently cupped her face, forcing her to look at him. 'If I'm honest with myself, I've loved you from the moment I glimpsed your long, shapely legs leaning out of the storage unit in the plane on the first day we worked together.'

He stroked a finger down the side of her face. 'You've filled my dreams, my waking thoughts. You've made me laugh and cry, but most importantly you've woken me up. I don't just exist any more. With you I truly live.'

His gaze dazzled her with love and at that precise moment she knew she wasn't a consolation prize. He loved her and she belonged in his heart.

'Will you marry me and be a mentor and friend to my daughter?'

Her heart exploded with joy. 'I think that is the most wonderful question I've ever been asked.'

His eyes twinkled. 'Yes, but do you have an answer?'

She laughed and placed her lips against his, seeking entry to his mouth, giving her answer to him and part of herself.

He kissed her back, long and hard, pledging love, friendship and security, all tied up with a swirling passionate heat.

She reluctantly pulled away, catching her breath.

He gave his wicked laugh. 'We've got the rest of our lives for kisses like that in less public places.' He grabbed her hand.

'Come on, let's go and celebrate our engagement with our daughter, and she can toast us with a blue heaven milkshake.'

Our daughter. Her dream had come true. 'That sounds like a perfect idea.'

His smile rained down on her like sunshine from a cloudless sky. 'Oh, and by the way, good luck talking Sasha out of a pink or purple bridesmaid's dress.'

She raised her brows. 'Pink saved us today so I think it should become our signature colour. Besides, a pink shirt under your tuxedo would look exceedingly good.'

A look of horror streaked across his face. 'There's no way known that I'm—'

She stole his argument with a kiss.

And he didn't object at all.

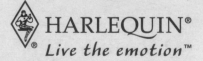

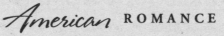
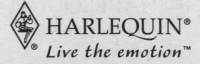

HARLEQUIN®
INTRIGUE®

BREATHTAKING ROMANTIC SUSPENSE

Shared dangers and passions lead to electrifying romance and heart-stopping suspense!

Every month, you'll meet six new heroes who are guaranteed to make your spine tingle and your pulse pound. With them you'll enter into the exciting world of Harlequin Intrigue— where your life is on the line and so is your heart!

THAT'S INTRIGUE—
ROMANTIC SUSPENSE
AT ITS BEST!

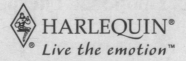

HARLEQUIN®
Live the emotion™

HARLEQUIN®

Super Romance®

...there's more to the story!

Superromance.
A *big* satisfying read about unforgettable characters. Each month we offer *six* very different stories that range from family drama to adventure and mystery, from highly emotional stories to romantic comedies—and much more! Stories about people you'll believe in and care about. Stories too compelling to put down....

Our authors are among today's *best* romance writers. You'll find familiar names and talented newcomers. Many of them are award winners— and you'll see why!

If you want the biggest and best in romance fiction, you'll get it from Superromance!

Exciting, Emotional, Unexpected...

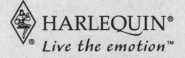

HARLEQUIN®
Live the emotion™

www.eHarlequin.com

HSDIR06